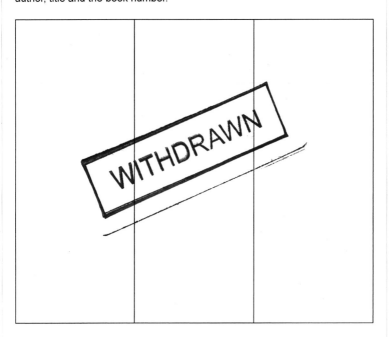

For Nicola – JIM

For Varvara, my beloved cat who has now gone Beyond – OLIA

Farshore

First published in Great Britain 2021 by Farshore
An imprint of HarperCollins*Publishers*
1 London Bridge Street, London SE1 9GF

farshore.co.uk

HarperCollins*Publishers*
1st Floor, Watermarque Building, Ringsend Road, Dublin 4, Ireland

Text copyright © Jim Beckett 2021
Illustrations copyright © Olia Muza 2021
Jim Beckett and Olia Muza have asserted their moral rights.

Text design by Janene Spencer

ISBN 978-1-4052-9828-5

Printed in Great Britain by CPI Group
1

Stay safe online. Farshore is not responsible for content
hosted by third parties.

MIX
Paper from
responsible sources
FSC® C007454

This book is produced from independently certified FSC™ paper
to ensure responsible forest management.

For more information visit: www.harpercollins.co.uk/green

JIM BECKETT

ILLUSTRATED BY OLIA MUZA

PART ONE

BEFORE

1

3:57 a.m. THURSDAY

30 hours and 3 minutes until Eternal Damnation

I knew my grandparents had been ill, but I hadn't expected them to explode. Not all on the same night anyway.

Pops went off first, with a bone-rattling blast that rocked the caravan and echoed across the moonlit moor. He was in the loo at the time – *Boom!* – right in the middle of a wee.

Gran blew up next, before I had a chance to rub the sleep out of my eyes. She went into the tiny toilet and did such a big *BOOM* that I fell out of my bunk bed.

Green smoke seeped round the edges of the bathroom door. When I saw Grandpa shuffling towards it, I leapt into action, determined to prevent any more grandparents from exploding.

'Noooooo!!! Grandpa! Don't GOOOO!!!'

Except I couldn't actually *leap* because the zip on my sleeping bag was stuck, so I had to squirm to the loo like a desperate caterpillar – and as soon as Grandpa tinkled, I was thrown back by the biggest *BOOM* yet.

For a moment, the world was strangely silent. Apart from the smoke and the lack of grandparents, everything in the caravan looked normal. Neatly folded bedding, half-finished crossword, tea-stained mugs stacked by the sink . . .

'Peepo!'

Malcolm's grinning face popped out the top of Nana's wheelie bag like a cheeky bargain from Meg's Mini Mart. The first time he did this, we all thought it was hilarious – but he'd hidden in "Nana wee-wee gag" about a thousand times since Monday, and the joke had lost its edge. Still, it was a relief to see my little brother hadn't exploded too. Mum and Dad would've been furious.

('Don't get into trouble – *and keep an eye on Malcolm!*' That was Mum when they dropped us off on Sunday night. 'Be good for your grandparents, do your homework – *and look after your little brother!*' That was Dad. No '*Have fun!*' or '*Enjoy your holiday!*' Not that there was much danger of that.)

'Pop BAM! Gam BAM! Gampa BAM!' said Malcolm, summarising the main events of the last twenty minutes as he hugged his Diddy Dino.

'Yeah,' I said. 'They did.'

He'd had an eventful week for a sixteen-month-old. On Monday, a dog stole our picnic. On Tuesday, an ant crawled on to his knee. On Wednesday, he lost a sock. So far, Malcolm seemed to be coping pretty well with tonight's exploding grandparents catastrophe. It had taken him much longer to get over the 'woof-woof num-num nic-nic' incident.

When I finally managed to escape from my sleeping bag, I tiptoed towards the toilet.

'Grandpa?' I whispered. 'Gran? Pops? Nana?'

I gently pulled the door (the lock hadn't worked for years) and peered in, afraid of the mess I might find. But the loo was empty. No splattered flesh, no smouldering slippers, no charred pyjamas. Nothing but hot smoke and a disturbing pong.

My grandparents had vanished.

Suddenly, I heard a rattling behind me. Someone –

or some*thing* – was trying to break into the caravan! But what kind of maniac would be lurking on a lonely moor at midnight? What kind of *monster* would attack a child whose grandparents had just exploded?

I scrabbled about for a weapon, grabbing the first thing I could find. Whatever was jiggling that rusty door was about to get whacked with a rolled-up *Risborough Gazette*. Pops and Grandpa always complained the local newspaper was covered in adverts – it would soon be covered in blood and guts!

My heart was thumping. The longer I waited, the less confident I felt about the *covered in blood and guts* idea. Maybe a few nasty bruises would be enough to get the message across. Some stern words might even do the trick. After all, it was half-term. I was meant to be relaxing, not slaying Hell Beasts.

Also, I couldn't help worrying that an epic battle would be quite noisy. Bloodcurdling screams risked drawing attention to the fact that I spent my holidays in the creepy abandoned caravan on the edge of the village – and *then* someone might find out that the creepy abandoned caravan wasn't really abandoned at all. My grandparents lived here, all four of them squashed in together.

Well, they used to.

The door rattled violently. This Hell Beast wasn't going away, so I'd have to wreak havoc whether I felt like it or not.

4

I raised the rolled-up *Risborough Gazette*, ready to strike . . .

The door burst open, and moonlight flooded the caravan.

'Aaaaaggghhhh!!!!' I yelled, lunging at the vicious fiend in its dressing gown and slippers . . . 'Nana?'

'Hello, Harley,' said Nana. 'Did I wake you? Sorry. This door keeps sticking – needs a drop of oil.'

I caught my breath and lowered my weapon. *THREE* explosions, *FOUR* grandparents: I still had one left! What a relief! And what terrible counting! Must've been the adrenaline.

'I popped out to get a closer look at the moon,' said Nana, stepping into the caravan. 'One last look at the beautiful night sky before . . . Oh!'

Her voice cracked as she noticed the empty beds.

'They went without me!'

2

4:34 a.m. THURSDAY

29 hours and 26 minutes until Eternal Damnation

'Pop BAM! Gam BAM! Gampa BAM!' said Malcolm, updating Nana on what she'd missed.

'That wasn't your grandparents going BAM,' said Nana, as we sat down on her creaky bed. 'That BAM was the sound of the Portal of Doom slamming shut behind them. Grandpa and Gran and Pops have *passed through,* that's all. Gone *Beyond.* It was their time.'

Nana stared at the smoking toilet.

'It'll be mine soon,' she said, gripping my hand as Malcolm curled up between us. 'But before I go, I have one final story to tell you.'

I shuffled into a comfortable position. My grandparents always did this – told one of their stories instead of just saying what they meant. Once upon a time, I used to love their crazy tales of Legendary Heroes and Mythical Monsters. But I'd heard them all about a zillion times now, and I couldn't help feeling they were slightly *pointless.* We lived in Kesmitherly! The closest anyone round here had come to Legendary Heroism was the time when Billy Jessop got his foot stuck in a drain and Janet the Lollipop Lady poked him free with her stripy stick.

Besides, the Legendary Heroes and Mythical Monsters in my grandparents' stories weren't even proper ones anyone had heard of. None of them were in that book Mum and Dad bought me – *The Big Book of Legendary Heroes and Mythical Monsters from All Myths and Legends All Over the World Ever.* And when I checked online, they weren't there either – not *one,* on the whole of the internet. They were *fake myths*!

'No road led to the caravan, and no one could remember how it got there,' Nana whispered, dramatically.

'Caravan?' I said, sitting up. 'You mean *this* caravan?'

Nana nodded.

Okay – this was something new. Maybe this story was going to be useful, after all.

'From a distance,' Nana continued, 'the caravan looked like it was growing out of the ground. Weeds overwhelmed the wheels and coiled round the axle, tethering it to the heath. But the raging winds fought to uproot it and set it free! Undergrowth and elements were locked in an eternal battle that neither could win, for the grasping grasses had no more hope of dragging the caravan into the bowels of the earth than the gusts and gales had of launching it to the heavens!'

This was classic Nana. She loved setting the scene and building suspense. Usually, I didn't mind her long descriptions of gloomy landscapes full of mist and shadow because I knew that soon enough Grandpa would jump in, getting way too excited about some Legendary Hero's peculiar childhood and enchanted weapons. Then Pops would pick up the tale, snarling and roaring and terrifying me with monsters that got bigger and scarier every time until I had to hide, giggling, behind a cushion (when I was little, I mean). But the more menacing Pops made the monsters, the tougher Gran would make the Legendary Hero! She'd get that fire in her eyes, and the Hero would come back fighting, summoning up strength from hidden depths . . . And on they'd go, all four of them weaving in and out of each other's stories, like they were separate parts of the same mad adventure.

But this wasn't that kind of story – and Pops and Gran and Grandpa were gone – and right now, I didn't have time for Nana's poetical scene-setting. I needed to know what was happening right here, right now, in real life.

I needed *facts*. What was a *Portal of Doom?* Where was *Beyond* . . .?

But Nana was on one of her Epic Pauses now, staring out of the window at the moonlit moor, while Malcolm slept peacefully between us. I turned my phone on to check the time – 04:55 – then turned it off again to save the battery. (There was no electricity in the caravan.) The moon tiptoed away; the sun peeped over the horizon . . .

Suddenly, Nana leapt off the bed, opened a cupboard, and rummaged. At last, some action! I tried to see past her, eager to get a glimpse of whatever magical heirloom she was searching for. A mystical pendant? An ancient scroll? An enchanted talisman?

'Teabags, good, plenty of teabags,' she muttered. 'Tea, tea, tea and . . . biscuits!' She bent down and opened the icebox. 'Milk – oh! Look at that!' she said, thrusting a nearly empty bottle into my face. 'There's only enough for one cup of tea, Harley! *One cup!*'

'I could go to the shop?' I suggested.

'Yes! Yes!' said Nana. 'Please. As soon as it opens, you must go.'

She took a chocolate biscuit from the cupboard and held it out to me.

'Harley, please take this biscuit. Consider it . . . a goodbye gift.'

'Because you're going *Beyond* too?' I asked.

9

Nana nodded, smiling sadly as I took the biscuit.

'Could you at least finish the story?' I asked, desperate to hold on to my last grandparent for as long as possible. 'It's only just begun.'

'*Yours* has, Harley,' she said, gazing wistfully out of the window. 'But mine . . .'

'Please, Nana?' I begged.

Nana turned to me decisively.

'I will finish my story. But first, there are things you must understand.' She brushed a crumb off the bed and shuffled up next to me. 'We are *Visionaries,* Harley. You, me, Pops, Malcolm, Gran, Grandpa. Even your parents. We can all see dead people.'

I stopped nibbling and lowered my biscuit.

'*I* can't see dead people,' I said.

'Harley, listen to me. This is important.' Nana gripped my hands in hers. 'Did you ever think it was strange that all your grandparents chose to live together in an old caravan upon the heath, so far from another Living Soul?'

I didn't know what to say to that. *Everything* my grandparents did was strange, and the caravan wasn't *far enough* from other Living Souls. It was only ten minutes outside the village. Half the kids at my school went past it on the bus.

'We live here,' said Nana, 'to help Restless Souls pass *Beyond* – from this life to the next! Some call us the

Gatekeepers of North-East Biddumshire . . . But that's mainly them lot over in Risborough. Round here, we're more often known as the Gatekeepers of Kesmitherly.'

'Woof-woof! Nic-nic!' squealed Malcolm, kicking wildly in his sleep.

Nana ignored him. She was very excitable.

'Our Duty,' she declared, 'is to protect and serve . . .'

She gestured towards the toilet.

'. . . this *Portal of Doom!*'

3

5:46 a.m. THURSDAY

28 hours and 14 minutes until Eternal Damnation

'My parents were Gatekeepers,' said Nana, 'as their parents had been Gatekeepers before them, and their parents before them – back and back into the distant past. From the day I was born, I knew that I too would become a Gatekeeper, guiding Restless Souls *Beyond*. But when I was seventeen, something happened which would change the course of my destiny. Our Portal became automated!'

'Autom—?'

'We were replaced, Harley – by a *machine*. Our Gatekeeping Duties were no longer required.'

Malcolm flapped and burbled and said, 'Diddy.'

'My parents retired, and my brothers got normal jobs,' Nana continued. 'But I didn't want any of that. So I left home, and I walked the earth. For I had a calling – to seek out other Portals and fulfil my destiny as a Visionary Gatekeeper.'

'In a caravan outside Kesmitherly?' I asked.

'I crossed oceans and deserts,' said Nana. 'Rivers and mountains. I visited many, many Portals. Some were hidden in mysterious caves overlooking the wild ocean; some were buried beneath ancient ruins, choked by creepers in the depths of the jungle; some were locked away in lavishly ornate shrines in forgotten cemeteries. I searched, and I searched. But none of these Portals required a new Gatekeeper. Many had become automated, like ours. Some had even been decommissioned.'

'Decom—?'

'Closed down, Harley! Automation was making the movement of Restless Souls so efficient that these Portals were considered unnecessary. But it's not right, if you ask me – passing *Beyond* without any human contact . . .'

'Didn't you miss home?'

'I *did* miss home! So much! So many times, I was ready to give up and go back. Then I met your grandpa.' Nana smiled a great big smile. 'I'd been so lonely, floating about on the endless ocean on my little raft. Then one day, another little raft bumped into mine, and the handsome young man on board got his paddle tangled up in my fishing net. He apologised, but I was glad of the company – and as we drifted along, we chatted away in the Language of the Dead.'

'The Language of the Dead?'

Nana nodded. 'It's how all Souls communicate – down there. But Visionaries can speak it too, even before we go *Beyond*. Like you and me are doing now.'

'I'm not speaking the Language of the De— Whoa!' I gasped, as I heard the strange sounds coming out of my mouth. 'I did *not* know I could do that.'

'Don't worry,' said Nana. 'Non-Visionaries don't even notice you're doing it. Anyway, we chatted, your grandpa and I, and it turned out he also came from a family of Visionary Gatekeepers, just like me. And he'd left *his* home to seek out a Portal of Doom, just like me! As we talked, our thoughts turned away from the past, towards the future – and we decided to continue our search together. A few months later, we found our new home, right here.'

'In Kesmitherly?!' I said. 'When you had the whole world to choose from? Ornate palaces with ocean views and mermaid lagoons and all that?'

'In Kesmitherly,' said Nana, 'we finally found what we'd been searching for. A Portal of Doom in need of

Gatekeepers. Biddumshire was drizzly, and grey, and not always very welcoming. But we had each other, and we had our destiny. When we first arrived, the old Gatekeeper was still here. But he was very ancient, and he had no family. We just had to wait for him to pass *Beyond* and the Portal of Doom would be ours.

'While we waited, we found work in the sauce factory just outside Risborough. Imagine our surprise at meeting another Visionary Couple on our first day there! Yes, your Gran and Pops had arrived only a week before us. Our destiny had summoned us here, all four of us – to become the new Gatekeepers of Kesmitherly *together*! Ah, such happy times we had, bottling Grimston's Sweet Relish and swapping stories of the Dead we'd known.

'The years passed, and the old Gatekeeper didn't die. Your mother was born. Your father was born. As they grew to adulthood, they became closer and closer. Oh, they had so much in common, your mum and dad! They both worked in offices, they both loved DIY, they could both see dead people . . . They married at Risborough Town Hall, on a beautiful grey day in November. A few years later, they had a child. A daughter.'

At last, we'd got to the part where I was born. Only twelve more years to go.

'Shortly after your birth, the old Gatekeeper passed *Beyond*. He was 116. Finally, we could retire from the sauce factory, and live together in this caravan – as the Gatekeepers of Kesmitherly!'

Nana took my hand and led me to the chemical toilet.

'We've had a few good years as Gatekeepers of this Portal of Doom. But now our time has come. And soon, all this will be yours.'

Nana gestured towards the loo, as if she was showing me the family jewels.

'So this is . . . not . . . a toilet?' I asked.

'This is a Portal of Doom. A gateway between this Life and *Beyond*. That which we call Death.'

'But I've . . . I mean we've all, you know . . . This isn't a campsite. There aren't any other facilities . . .'

'Oh, it's a toilet as well. It has a double function.'

'Right. And it's . . . mine?'

Nana beamed proudly and nodded. 'You are twelve years old, Harley. It is time.'

'Okay. Thank you for the biscuit. I don't think I want the spooky toilet though.'

'It is your destiny.'

'Why?' I asked. 'Why don't Mum and Dad take over?'

'They've already got jobs. And you know what they're like. They're always so busy. *You* are the new Gatekeeper, Harley!'

It was a lot to take in. As I watched Nana folding her duvet, I tried to get everything straight in my head, but all the Souls and Visionaries kept swirling about like a ghostly whirlpool. Then Nana lifted Malcolm out of the way so we could rig up her creaky little bed into a creaky little table. As she placed him on a pillow in the corner, his eyelids flickered sleepily.

'Arwee?' he murmured.

'I'm here, Maccy, it's okay,' I replied, and he rolled over and went back to sleep, squeezing Diddy Dino's neck.

'I'll try to hold on to show you your Duties,' said Nana, as we twisted and folded the bedtable. 'Just don't forget the biscuits. Also, they're each allowed one item of hand luggage. For snacks, magazines, anything they like, really. Last week, a Restless Soul took his pet parrot through purgatory! Although it's not a good idea for a living creature to pass through. Not good at all . . .'

Nana was full of nervous energy, like a queue for a zipwire. She fussed about, plumping up cushions and lining up the rug. Then she stood back and said: '*It is time!* Would you mind popping to the shop, Harley? We'll need two large bottles of milk.'

My head was so full of questions, I didn't know where to start. So I just got dressed, figuring the fresh air might do me good.

'If you run like the wind, you'll be there for when it opens,' said Nana, handing me her purse. 'I'll hold on for as long as I can, but hurry back! Just in case.'

Then Nana gave me the biggest, squeeziest hug ever, and I jumped out of the caravan and ran across the heath.

4

7:18 a.m. THURSDAY

26 hours and 42 minutes
until Eternal Damnation

Over the moor and down the road to Kesmitherly, I thought about everything Nana had told me. In the cold morning light, it all seemed very unlikely. If my grandparents really *were* the Gatekeepers of a Portal of Doom, why had they never mentioned it before? Why had Mum and Dad never brought it up? Then again, Pops, Gran and Grandpa had gone *somewhere* in a puff of smoke ...

As I jogged into the village, the nagging sounds of reality barged their way into my earholes, pushing aside all thoughts of Portals and Visionary Destinies.

'Hey! Harley! Harley!'

I hurried on with my head down, pretending not to notice the friendly girl shouting at me from the pub.

'Harley! Hey, Harley!' she called. *'Harley!'* – getting louder – *'HARLEY!'* – until she was too loud to ignore. I looked up at her smiling face, beaming at me through the open window of the Ragged Goose.

'Hi, Bess,' I mumbled.

'How's your half-term?' Bess asked. 'Hey, wait up! I'll come out!'

'All right,' I said, edging away, slowly, sort of half waiting, but still on my way to the shop.

Bess came bounding through the pub door and bounced up to me. 'Hey, Harley! What you up to today? Wanna go Splash Madness?'

I froze, trapped by her friendliness.

'Sorry, I . . . milk.' I shrugged. 'Bye!'

I ran across the road, escaping into Meg's Mini Mart. Inside, I ducked along the toothpaste and bleach aisle, and peeped over a toilet-roll display. Through the window, I could see her. Sitting on a bench outside the pub, swinging her legs. Smiling. Waiting.

Bess had moved to Kesmitherly a week earlier when her mums took over the Ragged Goose. She'd joined my class on the last day of term, and she'd been friendly ever since.

It was a nightmare.

In fairness, it wasn't *entirely* Bess's fault; she couldn't help being friendly. But I really couldn't risk getting caught up in all that friendship madness again. Not after Olly.

I peeped over the toilet rolls at Bess, still sitting, still waiting. It felt a bit mean, hiding from her. Maybe I should go over . . .?

I began to stand, then ducked down again.

Life was safer without friends. Recently, I'd been spending a lot of time helping my parents with chores and DIY – mainly to try and get back into their Good Books after all the Bad Times when Olly had been around. It was boring, but at least it was safe. The worse that can happen with DIY is you accidentally saw your leg off or nail your arm to a wall or electrocute yourself. Much less risky than friendship.

But as I looked over at Bess, casually throwing gravel into a hanging basket, I wondered . . . Maybe an *un*-imaginary friend might be okay? It would certainly be good to have someone to talk to about all the exploding-magic-toilet stuff. Maybe I *should* go to –

Wait a minute – *where* had she invited me? Did she say Splash Madness? SPLASH MADNESS!? What kind of person would invite *anyone* to Splash Madness? Was *she* mad? Was she joking? Had she even *seen* last month's report in the *Risborough Gazette*?

DEATH SLIDE NIGHTMARE

A spokesperson for Biddumshire Council has condemned Splash Madness as 'the most dangerous water park in the county', after a local resident nearly lost a thumb on one of the flumes.

In an exclusive interview with the *Risborough Gazette*, Micky Binston, 11, described his traumatic ordeal.

'The water was rushing up my trunks so fast it made my bum feel funny,' said Micky, a student at St Clotilde's Academy. 'When I reached round the back to adjust things, my thumb got bent. I haven't been able to play the kazoo since.'

The victim's mother, Sandra Binston, spoke of the family's distress.

'Micky used to be such a talented musicia'

Supposedly, they'd fixed it since then – but they would say that, wouldn't they? And anyway, even if they *had* fixed it, anyone with any sense could've seen this was an accident waiting to happen. The trouble with flumes is you've got no control. Once you're on, you just hurtle down and down and round and round, pointlessly, until you reach the end – and pray you've still got all your thumbs. I had nothing against water danger where you *were* in control, like when Miss Delaporte told us to jump in the deep end in our pyjamas to rescue a plastic brick. That was a risk worth taking. A *sensible* risk.

But random, unnecessary danger, where you just *let go* . . .

That was just silly.

Eventually, Bess's mum called her from an upstairs window, and Bess went back inside. I quickly bought the milk. On my receipt it said the time was 07:52, which was ridiculous. Because if it really *was* 07:52 . . .

I'd been hiding for twenty minutes!

I ran out of the shop, past the Ragged Goose, down the lane, over the moor, and into the caravan on the edge of Kesmitherly.

On the table was a note.

To Harley and Malcolm,
Sorry we didn't get to say a proper
goodbye, but my time has come.
I'll miss you. Look after each other.
Love Nana x

P.S. Please water the cactus

The toilet door was swinging in the breeze. Green smoke snaked out of the skylight.

Nana was gone.

But there wasn't time to be sad. Not yet. Before I could grieve for any of my grandparents, I had a problem to deal with.

Because Nana's wheelie bag was gone too. And Malcolm was nowhere to be seen.

5

8:05 a.m. THURSDAY

25 hours and 55 minutes
until Eternal Damnation

I turned my phone on and stared at it.

What could I say? How could I tell Mum that I'd let Malcolm pass through the Portal of Doom in Nana's wheelie bag? How could I tell Dad that I'd broken my promise to look after my little brother? How could I ever tell either of them that their favourite child had gone to the Land of the Dead *as hand luggage*?

A knock at the door made me jump.

I put my phone down and counted grandparents on my fingers: Pops, Gran, Grandpa, Nana. Definitely none left to sneak up on me.

Grabbing my rolled-up *Risborough Gazette* in both hands, I kicked open the door.

On the moor before me stood the biggest man I'd ever seen. His shirt clung to his belly like play dough wrapped in cling film, and he was sweating like crazy – presumably from the effort of not bursting out of his clothes.

'Hullo, pet,' said the clammy giant in a voice like friendly gravel. 'Sorry I'm late. You the new chief now, are you? Your grandparents passed through? Looked like they were about to, yesterday. I said to myself, "They look like they're about to pass through!" Yesterday I said that. I'm BK, by the way. We've not met before because you're usually asleep when I call, but I'm BK.'

'Hi, I'm Harl*aaaagghh*!!!'

I ducked as he swung an enormous fist at me.

'Fancy finding one of those in there!' he chuckled, producing a jelly bean from my ear. I took the jelly bean and breathed deeply. All this Land of the Dead stuff had really put me on edge.

'Pleased to meet you, Harl*aaagh*!' said BK. 'Right, I'm gonna sing the next bit because I always sing this bit, so I'm gonna sing it like usual. Okay?'

I nodded. BK cleared his throat and sang:

> '*Only four to-ooo-oo-oo-oooooo-*
> *ooo-ooo-day!*
> *Four Restless Souls of the Hesitant*
> *Dead . . .!*
> *Delivered to you-oo-ooo-oo!*
> *Get on board, get on board, get on*
> *bo-o-o-oard!*'

Now he was shaking violently, and I started to panic that he was about to explode too – until I realised he was sprooting or flonking or some other olden-days dance. When he'd finished, he leaned on the doorframe, breathing heavily.

As he recovered from his performance, I looked at the coach parked up on the moor behind him. There was something oddly familiar about it, like I'd seen it before, though I couldn't think where. It was old and battered and rusty, and it *shimmered* in a . . . well, in a *ghostly* way. Inside, four passengers were waiting patiently, as if they'd just stopped for petrol. Were these *Restless Souls*? Could I *really* see dead people?

'I know what you're wondering,' said BK when he'd got his breath back. 'How did a big lad like me learn to sing like that?'

'Actually, that's not exactly what I was wondering . . .'

'I'll tell you all about it sometime, but right now we'd

best crack on. I'm running late this morning, and I sincerely apologise for that. I'm afraid to say we've got some *very* Hesitant Dead with us today: some of this lot would *not* get on board! – Hey, are you all right, pet?'

'Mm-hm,' I lied.

BK peered at me, his head glistening in the morning sun as tiny streams of sweat gathered in his eyebrows. He seemed concerned, or suspicious, or hay-feverish.

'Did your grandparents go off peaceful like?' he asked.

'It was kind of noisy,' I said.

'Yeah, it does tend to be noisy. But it sounds worse than it is – so I've been told. Still, all four in one night. That's rough.'

He dabbed his head with a sleeve and looked towards the caravan.

'What's the little feller up to? Playing with his dinosaur, is he? Me and Malcolm often have a chat with Diddy Dino while your grandparents sort out the Souls and you're sleeping in your bed. Oh yes, we're right pals, me and your brother – Hey, are those tears, pet? Are you crying?'

'No,' I sniffed.

And then it all burst out – like it does when all the sadness and worry and panic and guilt is bubbling away until someone is unexpectedly kind, and you just can't hold it in any more. I told BK how Malcolm had gone through the Portal of Doom in Nana's wheelie bag, and how it was all my fault because I was hiding in Meg's Mini Mart when I should've been running like the wind . . . And if I'd got back sooner, I could've said a proper goodbye to Nana, and we'd have noticed Malcolm wasn't asleep in the corner, and I'd have guessed he was hiding in her bag waiting to say 'Peepo!' and I could've saved him from going *down there* . . .

And then BK was welling up, and he said what a good lad Malcolm was, and what a tragedy it was for an Innocent Soul to pass through before his time – and that made me cry even more, and I think BK cried too, but it could've been hay fever or sweat.

'So what you gonna do, pet?' said BK, when we'd both pulled ourselves together.

'Don't know,' I said. 'Call my parents, I guess.'

I kicked thoughtfully at a clump of heather. I still couldn't imagine *ever* talking to Mum and Dad about all this.

'I just wish there was some other way,' I said. 'Like, if only I could just . . . I dunno, go through the Portal of Doom myself and *rescue* him . . .'

'Why not?' said BK, checking his watch. 'That's not a bad idea, that is.'

I stared at him in disbelief. 'Seriously?' I said. 'But is it even possible?'

'It's gotta be worth a shot,' said BK. 'Seeing as you're

a Visionary and all that gubbins. You never know – this might be your destiny.'

I glanced behind me at the Portal of Doom. If there was a chance, even a *tiny chance* of getting Malcolm back . . . But a rescue mission into the underworld? It sounded so dramatic. So attention-seeking.

'Only issue would be getting back out again,' said BK. 'I mean, if you *did* fancy a crack at it, you'd want to avoid getting stuck. You know, trapped. *FOREVER!!!* You know, like, *ENTOMBED FOR ALL TIME IN THE LAND OF THE DEAD!!!!* I'm talking about, you know . . . *ETERNAL DAMNATION!!!!!* You'd want to avoid that.'

'Yeah,' I said. 'I'd want to avoid that.'

'Poor little lad!' said BK. 'It's not natural, is it? A Living Soul going *Beyond* as hand luggage. He's like one of them poor spiders that pass through in a dead man's pocket.'

I looked over at the passengers on the coach who were still just sitting there, looking bored and disappointingly unghostly.

'Do you think we could get one of them to take *me* through in a bag?' I whispered.

BK shook his head. 'No offence, pet, but you're a bit *long* for hand luggage. I reckon your best bet is to try and pass through the same way they do.'

'Right,' I said. 'Same way as the Restless Souls . . . And how's that, then?'

BK was shocked. 'You're kidding me! Did your grandparents not explain your Basic Gatekeeper Duties?'

I shrugged. 'I think Nana was going to. She got kind of distracted.'

'What a family!' BK shook his head. 'Listen, pet. I'm no expert, but as far as I understand it, a Visionary Gatekeeper's main job is to make everyone a cup of tea.'

'I just make everyone a cup of tea?'

'That's right. Not ordinary teabags, mind – use the tin marked *Special Teabags*. Make a nice strong brew. Give everyone a cuppa. Make sure they drink it right down. Then, one by one, they pop in the loo – piddle, piddle, bang, bang – job done!'

'I just make all the Restless Souls of the Hesitant Dead a cup of tea?'

'*Special Tea*, yes. But don't worry about this lot.' He nodded to the four passengers on the coach behind him. 'They already know the drill. I explained it on the way over.'

'So. *Special Tea*, drink it down, go to the . . . *Portal of Doom* and that's it? And you reckon that'll work for me too? So I can go through and rescue Malcolm?'

'I reckon so, pet. But as for getting back OUT, and not getting *TRAPPED FOR ALL TIME IN ETERNAL DAMNATION*!!!! I'm afraid I wouldn't know about that sort of thing – not my area of expertise. Anyway, time really is cracking on, and I'm sorry to make you do this, pet – but you *are* the new Gatekeeper of Kesmitherly, and it *is* your Visionary Duty, so you'd better get this lot through.'

BK helped the passengers out of the coach and led them over the scrubby moor and into the caravan. First came an old lady in a cardigan, followed by another old lady in another cardigan. Next, a sad-looking teenager with a stick of candyfloss, and finally, a terrified firefighter who looked like he'd seen a ghost.

'Look, pet, I've got another pick-up I'm already late for,' said BK, tucking his shirt in. 'But hey – don't you worry, all right? He'll be okay, your brother. You just do what you have to do.'

'Thanks, BK,' I said, looking up at his kind, sweaty face, and feeling like we'd known each other for years, instead of minutes.

'I shouldn't really be doing this, you know,' he said, looking wistfully at the horizon. 'Motoring about at all hours, picking up Restless Souls and ferrying them to Portals of Doom. I should've been on telly! In the movies! But it's like me old mum used to say: "It's never too late!" She's dead now, so it's too late for her. Still, at least I've got me health!'

As BK launched into a fresh coughing fit, I waved goodbye and went into the caravan.

6

8:44 a.m. THURSDAY

25 hours and 16 minutes
until Eternal Damnation

Inside, the Restless Souls were squeezed round the caravan's tiny table. As soon as I came in, the conversation stopped and they all turned to stare at me. One of the old ladies scowled. The firefighter sniffled. The girl with the candyfloss sighed.

Then the other old lady smiled and told me what a lovely journey she'd had with such a friendly driver who'd even let them stop for a bun at Pickerton service station. And then she said, 'I'm sorry, dear, but would you mind? I rather need the toilet.'

'Not yet!' snapped the scowling old lady. 'You know

the rule, Doris! That awful driver sang it to us enough times. *Drink, drink, drink your tea! Then you'll be allowed a wee!'*

'You're right, Glenda,' said Doris, smiling and crossing her legs. 'I'm sorry.'

I found the tin labelled *Special Teabags,* filled the kettle, and lit the hob.

'So, er, cup of tea, anyone?' I asked.

'No! *Please, NO!'* yelled the firefighter and burst into tears.

'Okay . . .' I said. 'Anyone else?'

'Everyone!' snapped Glenda. 'Come on!'

As the water boiled, no one spoke. The firefighter sobbed loudly, Doris squirmed politely, and I tried to imagine following them through the Portal of Doom to rescue my brother from the Land of the Dead. I still couldn't get over how *dramatic* it sounded. But it was either that, or 'fess up to my parents . . .

I put a *Special Teabag* in each mug and poured boiling water on top. I added a splash of milk and dunked and squeezed the teabags with a spoon before removing them. The result certainly didn't *look* special. It looked like a hot muddy puddle, same as normal tea. I tried to sniff it, but the dead people were staring at me again.

I passed the mugs round. Doris, the nice old lady, took a sip and stood up.

'All of it!' snapped Glenda. *'Drink, drink, drink your tea!'*

Then Doris downed the whole steaming mugful and rushed to the loo. A moment later, she exploded. Sorry, not *exploded*. She *passed through*, and the Portal of Doom slammed shut behind her.

Green smoke wafted through the caravan, stinging our eyes. The firefighter was whimpering. The girl with the candyfloss was sighing and sighing like a deflating balloon. Glenda was moaning about the *shoddy furniture*, the *manky tea*, the *limited legroom*, and how they let *blooming anyone guide Restless Souls into the next life these days . . .*

'I can't do it!' sobbed the firefighter. 'I'm telling you, I can't do it. Don't make me do it, pleeeease! I won't do it, I won't drink my tea!'

These dead people were really starting to bug me. I needed to get rid of them so I could focus on psyching myself up to rescue Malcolm. But how? How could I get these stubborn Restless Souls to drink their tea?

Then it came to me, like a voice from *Beyond*.

'Don't forget the biscuits!'

Biscuits! *That's* how you make tea drinkable! I emptied a packet of chocolate biscuits on to a plate and put it on the table.

The firefighter stared at them, desperately trying to resist their chocolatey-biscuity aroma. He licked his lips. He clenched his fists and closed his eyes – but one eye peeped open. The candyfloss girl took a biscuit and ate it slowly. The firefighter drooled. Slowly, teasingly, Glenda dunked a biscuit in her tea and munched the sweet, soggy end . . . And the firefighter could resist no longer. He grabbed a handful of biscuits, drowned them in tea and shovelled them into his hungry mouth. He crunched and chewed and dunked and swallowed until the biscuits were gone. Then he stared at his empty mug and burst into tears.

Minutes later, he was drumming on the table, jiggling his legs and grinding his teeth.

'Somebody needs a pee pee!' taunted Glenda. 'Trickle, trickle, splash, splash. Sorry, does that make it worse?'

'I don't want to go!' the firefighter sobbed. 'I really don't want to go. But I can't hold on – *I've got to go!*'

He charged into the loo. *BOOM!* The caravan shook in a fresh cloud of green smoke.

Slowly, Glenda stood up and followed him through, muttering about *cheap crockery* and *lazy young people. BOOM!*

But the moody candyfloss girl was still sitting there, her tea untouched.

'Would you like some more milk?' I asked, sort of sweetly but through gritted teeth.

She sighed at me and rolled her eyes. 'I didn't even *want* to go on that lame rollercoaster. And then I fell out of it and died, and I only went on it because my lame friends told me to. And now I'm dead and it's put me right off my candyfloss.'

'But once you're *down there*,' I said, in my friendliest, sweetest voice, 'you'll have *infinite* candyfloss and everything you ever dreamed of, and no one will ever make you do anything ever again.'

Obviously, I had no idea if any of this was true, but it seemed to do the trick. The candyfloss girl sighed again, drank her tea, and passed sulkily into the next life through the caravan's chemical toilet.

I slumped into a chair, exhausted. This Gatekeeper job was a nightmare. No wonder Mum and Dad didn't want it. Still, I'd got through it – for today. My Visionary Duties had been fulfilled, the Restless Souls had passed through . . .

And now it was my turn.

I looked over at the still-smoking Portal of Doom. Was I seriously going to do this? Explode into the Unknown, all brave and reckless and attention-seeking? It didn't sound like me. It sounded so *risky*. And not a *sensible risk* like when Miss Delaporte got us to dive for a plastic brick in our pyjamas. This was an *insane risk*, like going to Splash Madness with Bess.

In fact, it was exactly the sort of stupidly brave thing one of those Legendary Heroes from my grandparents' stories would've done. They were always facing horrific danger and terrifying monsters – like when Bilbamýn the

Bold fought the Many-Limbed Optimugoon, or Vileeda the Valiant ambushed the Razor-Elbowed Glockenpard. But *they* had Great Courage and Massive Swords. I just had a rolled-up newspaper and some biscuits.

My phone buzzed with a message.

> hi Harley, is Malcolm OK? & everyone else? boiler went in nice & easy, will send a pic. Final coat 2day so c u 2moro morning at 10.00
>
> love Mum XXX

Tomorrow at 10am?! Well, that was that, then. There wasn't even *time* to go on a stupidly brave quest. I should call them, explain the situation.

Let Mum and Dad sort it out.

They'd know what to do.

The phone stared at me, tempting me to make the sensible choice.

But if I told them Malcolm had descended to the underworld while I was hiding in a shop, I'd never hear the end of it. *All we asked was for you to keep an eye on your brother! This is worse than the time you melted Mum's shoes! Worse than getting banned from ballet! Worse than what you did to those gnomes! And don't you go blaming 'Olly'. Looking after our favourite child was* your *responsibility,* not *your imaginary friend's!*

And even if I *could* tell them (which I couldn't), they'd be too busy for a rescue mission to the Land of the Dead, anyway. They were *always* busy, with their endless chores and DIY. And this week, they hadn't even wanted my help. Me and Malcolm had been packed off to the caravan for a "holiday" while they got on with some "big jobs". Well, I didn't need *their* help, either! I could wrestle Hell Beasts *by myself,* while they had fun plumbing in the new boiler and decorating the lounge!

I reached for a *Special Teabag* – and paused. What was I playing at, getting all determined and brave like some Fake Legendary Hero? I put the teabag back in the tin and picked up my phone. But as my thumb hovered over 'Mum', I froze.

Something was watching me.

Something . . . not . . . quite . . . *alive.*

There, in the corner, peeping out from behind a pillow, a pair of eyes stared at me accusingly.

I hadn't been prepared for this.

Every time I'd tried to convince myself that my brother would be okay in the underworld, I'd pictured him snuggled up with his favourite squidgy dinosaur. As long as he had Diddy Dino, Malcolm was fearless. Missing socks, exploding grandparents, ghostly coaches full of dead people – literally nothing bothered him.

But *without* Diddy . . .

On Monday, we'd gone to Frimpton and left his cuddly dinosaur behind. When a dog stole our picnic, everyone laughed – apart from Malcolm. Malcolm freaked out. He couldn't see the funny side of the 'woof-woof num-num nic-nic' incident until we were back at the caravan with Diddy.

That's how it always went. Without Diddy, Maccy couldn't cope. And right now, boy and dinosaur were separated by more than a short bus ride to our favourite seaside town.

Right now, Diddy was *up here*, staring at me.

And Malcolm was *down there*. Way beyond Frimpton. In a wheelie bag.

This was no time for an awkward phone call. This was a time for action. My brother must be reunited with Diddy Dino – even if it cost me my Soul.

I shoved the goggle-eyed dinosaur into my rucksack and boiled the kettle.

7

9:47 a.m. THURSDAY

24 hours and 13 minutes
until Eternal Damnation

I drank tea and ate biscuits and drank tea and ate biscuits and I replied to my mum.

> All good here. Having a great time!
>
> No rush for boiler pic. H xxx

Then I grabbed my maths book to write an action plan. But when I opened it, I saw the homework I hadn't done yet, and it made me sad because Gran *always* helped me with maths homework, and no one else explained it so clearly, and I missed all of them so much, and I wished they were here, and not even just to help with maths homework. Then I doodled a seahorse flying a kite (this was one of the Calming Strategies my counsellor showed me after all the stuff with Olly), and I wrote my action plan.

1. Pass through Portal of Doom
2. Find Malcolm
3. Return to caravan before 10:00 tomorrow morning
4. Try to get out of Gatekeeper of Kesmitherly job

CONCLUSION: Rescuing Malcolm from Land of the Dead = PROPER SCARY
(But better than a lifetime of lectures from Mum and Dad.)

I checked through the contents of my rucksack one final time: Phone, 54% battery – check. Hoodie, in case it's chilly in the Land of the Dead – check. Rolled-up *Risborough Gazette,* to be replaced by broadsword or magic staff at earliest convenience – check. Diddy Dino – check. Half a packet of biscuits – check. Maths book containing action plan – check.

And now, I could delay no longer. I'd watered the cactus. It was time.

I sat on the Portal of Doom, clutching my rucksack, staring at the fluffy hand towel in front of me. I was trembling – partly from the fear of passing through purgatory, the guilt of lying to my parents and the anxiety of failing in my quest – but mainly I was just buzzing from a mad sugar rush.

I'd eaten a lot of biscuits.

I'd drunk a lot of *Special Tea*.

It was time to release my destiny.

PART TWO

BEYOND

8

10:00 a.m. THURSDAY

24 hours until Eternal Damnation

I landed on my back with a damp thump and the Portal of Doom slammed shut above me. Slowly, I stood up and looked around. A greenish fog hid everything beyond the narrow ledge I'd landed on, but I could hear the roar of rushing water nearby. I pulled up my jeans and tightened the straps on my rucksack.

Suddenly, something hurtled towards me through the murky clouds. I hid my face and curled into a ball – but it stopped, just in front of me, and floated invitingly. It was a sink. I felt better after I'd washed my hands. No one wants to head out on an Epic Quest without washing their hands. Especially one that starts in a *Portal of Doom*.

As the sink flew away, another bulky object floated out of the mist. This was a newspaper stand, like the ones at the bus station where you can help yourself to a free copy of the *Risborough Gazette.*

INFORMATION FOR NEW ARRIVALS
Please Take a Brochure

But it was empty – there were no brochures left to take. Just my luck. The unhelpful stand drifted away, and I noticed another, smaller sound above the gushing roar.

Someone was crying.

The sobbing grew louder as I crawled along the slippery ledge, until I could see the outline of a familiar figure through the haze. It was the firefighter. He had his arms wrapped around a rock and was clinging on for dear life – which was a complete waste of time, given his total deadness. But when the mist cleared, I saw what he was crying about.

We were high. Too high. Crazily, perilously high. Mountain high. Aeroplane high. Moon high. I shut my eyes and took slow, deep breaths to stop my head spinning. There were no other rocks to cling to, and I felt like I was going to slide off the slippery ledge at any moment and plummet to my . . . doom? Damnation? Death? What exactly *would* I plummet to?

I didn't fancy finding out. And anyway, I didn't have to. There was another way down. A 'fun' way.

Between me and the firefighter, a torrent of yellow-green gloop frothed and foamed and roared down the steepest, fastest, scariest water slide anyone has ever seen, anywhere, ever.

'It's the Flume of Infinite Terror!' sobbed the firefighter, and the pink neon sign buzzing and flickering in the semi-darkness agreed:

THE FLUME OF INFINITE TERROR!!!
Please queue behind the line

'Doesn't look that bad,' I lied, without looking down.

The firefighter wailed.

And although he was one of the whiniest people I'd ever met, I couldn't blame him. The Flume of Infinite Terror looked approximately fourteen zillion times bigger and faster than the water slide in Splash Madness where Micky Binston nearly lost a thumb. And to make matters worse, the stuff going down it wasn't even water! It was a sort of thick gloop that would be *impossible* to swim in, and would probably drag us under like quicksand, and might even burn us like quicklime, and was going too fast like quickcustard.

However, unlike the famously dangerous water slide at Splash Madness, this flume wasn't pointless. It would still go round and round, and down and down – but then it would end up where I needed to get to, instead of back where I started. I'd almost certainly lose a thumb or two, but at least those thumbs wouldn't be sacrificed for nothing.

Unfortunately, none of this made it any less terrifying, and the firefighter was still blubbering away like a big baby.

'So, er, seen any good fires lately?' I asked, hoping a chat might calm us both down. (Doodling a seahorse just didn't feel like an option right now.)

The firefighter wailed some more, then snivelled, just to mix it up a bit.

'We could go together?' I suggested, bottom-shuffling towards him.

'Don't make me go down there. It's too steep. I don't like it! *Pleeeeease* don't make me go DOWN THERE!!!' he screamed.

'Hmm,' I said. 'But if we stay here, we'll be . . . here. Forever, presumably.'

He wailed even louder and clung to his rock even harder – and for a moment, I did think about leaving him there. I'd entered the Land of the Dead on an urgent brother-rescuing mission, so I really didn't have time for all this whingeing. On the other hand, abandoning a Soul in what I guessed was purgatory seemed a bit harsh.

There was no way round it. I needed to slide, and I needed to persuade old whingey-boots to slide too.

But how?

I guess if one of those Fake Legendary Heroes from my grandparents' stories had been in this situation, they'd have carried him to safety on an enchanted dolphin or an obliging albatross. But I needed a sensible, practical plan. And suddenly I remembered Miss Delaporte, and how she helped Kris, the most nervous boy in Year 5, overcome his fear of goggles.

'Look, there's a snake on the rock!' I shouted.

'Whaaaat?!?!?' squealed the firefighter – and as soon as he let go, I grabbed his ankles and leapt down the slide, dragging him with me.

'Noooooooooo!!!!' he screamed.

'Wahoo!' I yelled, twisting and turning, slipping and sliding, as I whooshed down the gloopy tunnel.

It was *fantastic*! Really, truly, THE BEST FLUME *EVER*!!! Even better, I imagined, than the water slides at Splash Madness or Froth City or Super Wet Land or even Bubbly Damp World in Frimpton! I was having a better holiday than my classmates, after all! Bet none of *them* had a Portal of Doom in their toilets!

'Wheeeee!' I hollered, shutting my eyes against the spray (and my mouth too when I remembered the Portal's "double function").

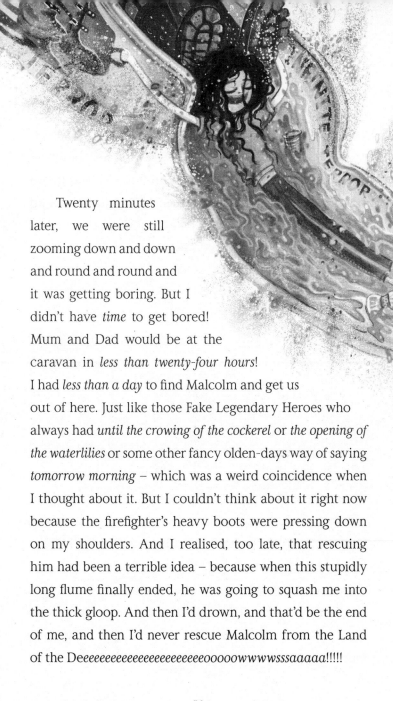

Twenty minutes later, we were still zooming down and down and round and round and it was getting boring. But I didn't have *time* to get bored! Mum and Dad would be at the caravan in *less than twenty-four hours*! I had *less than a day* to find Malcolm and get us out of here. Just like those Fake Legendary Heroes who always had *until the crowing of the cockerel* or *the opening of the waterlilies* or some other fancy olden-days way of saying *tomorrow morning* – which was a weird coincidence when I thought about it. But I couldn't think about it right now because the firefighter's heavy boots were pressing down on my shoulders. And I realised, too late, that rescuing him had been a terrible idea – because when this stupidly long flume finally ended, he was going to squash me into the thick gloop. And then I'd drown, and that'd be the end of me, and then I'd never rescue Malcolm from the Land of the Deeeeeeeeeeeeeeeeeeeeeeeeeoooooowwwwsssaaaaa!!!!!

53

The flume curved upwards and stopped, launching us high into the air – then falling, down, down, down – *KERSPLADGE!* – into a pool of oozing gunge . . . and still down, more slowly now, but still *DOWN*, deeper and deeper below the surface . . . lungs filling up with the thick yellow gloop of purgatory . . . drowning, in the sewage of human history.

9

10:48 a.m. THURSDAY

23 hours and 12 minutes
until Eternal Damnation

Come on, Harley. Come on, you can do this. Remember that plastic brick you rescued? You got a badge for it. That's it. Hold your breath . . . keep going . . . KICK!

I kicked and I flapped, but it was hopeless. The gloop was too thick, and we'd only ever been taught to swim in water. Even Alisha, the vice-captain of the Under 13s North-East Biddumshire Reserve Squad, could only swim in water. This was so *typical!* All that time learning to swim in *WATER*, and what good was it to me now? Why did school never teach us anything useful!?

But I didn't give up. I kept kicking, I kept flapping

– madly, hopelessly – like a hamster in porridge . . . I kept *trying* . . . And suddenly, I surfaced. Thrashing my arms and legs wildly, gasping for breath, I was keeping my head up – I was staying afloat – I was swimming. I was *SWIMMING*!!!

'I'm *SWIMMING*!' I spluttered. 'I'm *SWIMMING*!!! I can swim through the Gloop of Purgatory! I can swim through *ANYTHING*!!!'

Then I realised I was actually *standing*; the pool wasn't that deep.

I stopped flapping and waded to the side, hoping no one had noticed.

As I clambered out of the pool, the firefighter splashed up beside me. He was grinning from ear to ear, happy for the first time since I'd known him.

'That was *awesome*!' he yelled. 'That was the *BEST FLUME EVER*! Let's go again! I'm going again! Come on, let's do it again!'

While he ran off to find a way back up, I sat, dripping, and looked around at the underworld. The mist was less green down here, more beige. There were some plastic palm trees and a few deckchairs scattered around the splash pool. Apart from that, there wasn't a lot to see: no flames, no fluffy pink clouds, no rainbows, no eternal night, no Ice Palace. Just a lot of beige, and a weird indoor/outdoor vibe that made me wonder if I should take my shoes off.

'Told him he was better off dead,' grumbled a familiar voice. I turned to see Glenda and Doris, the old Restless Souls from that morning, sitting on a bench behind me. They were wearing bathrobes and slippers and had their hair wrapped in towels.

'Hello, Harley,' said Doris. 'Good journey?'

'Erm,' I said, wondering where they'd got their towels.

'We've got an *eternity* of this misery,' Glenda moaned.

'Don't be silly, Glenda,' said Doris. 'Someone'll come for us soon. The girl with the candyfloss was collected very promptly – by a *unicorn*!'

'It was a horse with an ice-cream cone taped to its head,' Glenda sneered. 'Mind you, it turned up a darned sight quicker than my Reg. He always was a slow old twit.'

The two old ladies looked so similar in their matching robes, with their soggy cardigans sagging over the bench between them; but while Doris was soft and comforting, like freshly baked bread, Glenda was like a wasp trapped behind glass.

'You can't get back out! One-way ticket down 'ere!' Glenda jeered at the firefighter, who had given up his search for steps and was now leaping about, trying to clamber *up* the flume. But it was way too high, and even if he could have reached, it would have been an impossible climb – the slide was too steep, and there was too much frothy, cascading gloop. But he kept on, leaping and leaping, until

57

three little rabbits hopped over and nuzzled his ankles.

'Sandi! Floella! Gary!' he squealed with delight, scooping the little bunnies into his big arms and burrowing his nose into their fluffiness. 'My *babies*! I thought I'd never see you again!'

'Lucky so-and-so,' muttered Glenda jealously as the firefighter turned his back on the flume and skipped joyously into the mist. 'Animals are more loyal than people!'

'Let's all just relax, shall we?' said Doris. 'Our Guides will be here soon. Probably got held up on the Road to Nowhere.'

'So are we *waiting* here?' I said.

'That's right, dear,' Doris replied. 'It's all explained in the Information Brochure. Didn't you get a chance to read yours on the way down the slide?'

'I didn't get one,' I said. 'They'd run out.'

'Oh, what bad luck!' said Doris. 'I'd lend you mine but I'm afraid I dropped it when I flew out the end. It must've sunk into the gloop. Glenda, perhaps you could lend Harley yours?'

'Ha!' sneered Glenda, covering the pocket of her robe as if she thought I might steal it.

I stared into the fog, thinking about all that precious *information* I didn't have. This was so *typical*! Here I was, with my twenty-four hours ticking away towards catastrophe just like those Fake Legendary Heroes. But unlike those Lucky Heroes, I didn't have a clue what to do next. See, those Heroes were always given valuable advice by a wise old mentor before setting off on a quest. Grandpa liked to do those bits – he'd go all wizened and croaky, pretending to be a sage or a sibyl or a soothsayer, and say things like, 'Never stroke the Badger of Claerbennon – even when it rolls on its back!' Where was *my* advice? I didn't even have a brochure.

I looked around our poolside waiting area. We were hemmed in by thick fog on every side – trapped – like depressed tourists in a rundown holiday resort. Tucked under a faded deckchair, a pair of miserable espadrilles lingered beside a lonely flip-flop. The plastic palm trees were covered in dust. One of them, behind the bench with the old ladies on, had a half-deflated blow-up toucan perched on it. Its great floppy beak drooped tragically, and I thought it might've been the saddest rubber bird I'd ever seen. Then Doris smiled at me with a look of gentle encouragement – and I pulled myself together and smiled back. Good old Doris. She was doing her best to help.

Wait a minute! *Doris, doing her best to help* . . . Of course! DORIS! She was *old*, she was *here* . . . and she'd read the Information Brochure! It made perfect sense: Doris was my mentor!

'You were just saying about the Road to Nowhere?' I said, eager to learn more from my wise adviser.

'I think that's probably it, over there,' said Doris, pointing to a dusty track leading off into the mist. 'Apparently it used to be bright yellow, but it hasn't been cleaned for centuries. It seems the Dead are a rather inefficient bunch.'

'Lazy, more like!' snapped Glenda. 'Worse than the Living!'

'So is that the right way to go?' I asked, looking at the dusty road. 'To Nowhere?'

'Where else you gonna go?' snickered Glenda. 'You either get off your bum and follow the Road to Nowhere, or you stay here – and still go nowhere!'

Glenda cackled away, and Doris shook her head disapprovingly.

'Yes, it is the right way, dear. But you can't go by yourself. You have to wait for your Guide.'

'My Guide?'

'It'll be someone special who's already passed *Beyond*. Usually a family member, or a friend, or a pet –'

'Or a useless waste-of-space idle old husband!' Glenda grumbled.

'That firefighter you came down with,' Doris continued, ignoring the interruption, 'was collected by his pet rabbits. The girl with the candyfloss galloped off on her unicorn –'

'Horse!'

'And Glenda's waiting for her husband, Reg. Who do you think your Guide might be?'

Immediately, I thought of Gran or Nana or Grandpa or Pops – or hopefully all of them. It *must* be them. They were the only dead people I knew, apart from Mr Purry Paws, our old cat.

But why weren't they here already?

In fact, thinking about it, Doris would've arrived not long after Nana – maybe she'd seen her! I turned excitedly to my wise mentor.

'Doris?' I said. But Doris wasn't listening. The pensioner was on the edge of her seat, squinting down the road at a figure striding out of the mist. As this person came into view, I recognised her immediately. It was Doris. The woman hurrying towards Doris was *Doris*! But a smaller, younger version . . .

'Mum!' gasped Doris, jumping to her feet.

'My little Doris! Sweetheart!' said Doris's mum, running up to her and pinching her elderly daughter's cheeks like she was a baby. 'My, haven't you grown!'

I watched as the pair of them walked off, arm in arm, chattering away. Doris was older than her own mother, but that didn't seem to matter down here. They'd found one another, and off they went. Heading Nowhere. Together.

I felt stupid for thinking Doris might've been my mentor. She wasn't wise, she was just polite. And now she'd gone, like everyone else, and it was just me and nasty old Glenda. I could understand why poor old Reg wasn't in a hurry to collect *her*. But why was *I* still here?

Where was *my* Guide?

10

11:27 a.m. THURSDAY

22 hours and 33 minutes
until Eternal Damnation

I pulled my socks up, tightened the straps on my backpack, and stared boldly into the mist.

I was ready; I had to be. I would find Malcolm, I would rescue him from Death, and I'd get us both Back to Life before ten o'clock tomorrow morning. And I'd do it without any help from anyone else. I'd got this far. I could do the Road to Nowhere by myself too.

I had enough time. I had enough biscuits. All I needed was courage, determination, resilience . . .

'Ha ha ha ha ha!'

I tried to ignore the miserable old woman laughing

behind my back, but it was no good. Glenda was only stating the obvious.

I wasn't a Legendary Hero.

I was just a girl with a rolled-up newspaper who didn't know what she was doing. I should never have come here.

Phlooomp!

Something landed on my back. Something warm and leathery. Something wobbly and moist. I tried to shake it off, and it held on more tightly. I breathed deeply, straining against the extra weight, and took a step towards the mist.

Phlooomp!

Another one jumped on, just above the first. This one was bigger, moister, leatherier. The size of a big wombat or a small armadillo. When I tried to flick them off, their claws dug into my hair. When I jumped and jiggled, their suction pads stuck more firmly to my shoulders. The more I tried to shake them off, the more they clung to me.

'Ha! What a pickle!' scoffed Glenda, hobbling over to interfere. 'Young lass like you shouldn't be bogged down with Regrets.'

'With what?' I asked.

'Regrets!' she declared, waving her Information Brochure at me impatiently. 'You've got a big pair of them on your back. Regrets cling to you, slow you down. You've got to try and shake them off.'

Shaking made it worse – I knew that. The harder I shook, the tighter they clung on.

I *knew* that.

But maybe Glenda knew something that I didn't. After all, she'd read the brochure. Maybe I'd misjudged her. Maybe *she* was my mentor! It sounded crazy, but the Portal of Doom was disguised as a caravan toilet. Perhaps my mentor was disguised as a mean and unhelpful person?

I tried jiggling once more, as vigorously as I could. The Regrets clung on even harder.

'I *knew* I shouldn't have listened to you!' I moaned. 'I *knew* they'd cling on harder! Why would I think you're trying to help me? No one's helping me!'

Phlooomp!

Another Regret flubbed on to me, attaching itself to my leg.

'Eughh!' I cried, flicking at its greasy knobbles. 'I shouldn't have listened to you, but I really shouldn't have *regretted* listening to you!'

PHLOOOOMP!!!

A Regret the size of a spaniel landed on my back and knocked me to the ground.

'My, what a biggun!' Glenda exclaimed. 'You've been got by the Regret of All Regrets. That's the biggest, squelchiest one of them all. The Regret that turns up when you start regretting regretting!'

The Regrets pinned me down. I couldn't move.

'Now listen to me, young lady!' Glenda scolded, waving her stick. 'You need to shake these Regrets off and look on the bright side. Go on, shake!'

'If I shake, they cling on harder!' I snapped.

'Typical young person, thinks she knows better than her elders! Don't know why I waste my breath –'

Phlooomp!

A blobby Regret leapt off my shoulder and landed on Glenda's head.

'I wish I'd never bothered hobbling over to you!' the old lady whined on.

Another Regret slopped off me and slapped across Glenda's shoulders like a blubbery shawl.

'Ooh, I never should've married Reg, he was nothing but trouble!' moaned Glenda.

One by one, the slobbery Regrets detached themselves from me and sailed across to the old woman. Each time, I caught a glimpse of their shiny underbellies – *the bright side* – just as Glenda had suggested. The Regrets splurped and slopped, until they swamped the miserable pensioner, and I could move freely once again.

Only one little Regret remained. It perched on my shoulder like a spiteful parrot, whispering in my ear: *'Should've kept an eye on your brother, kept an eye on your brother, an eye on your brother, your brother, your brother, your brother . . .'*

I ignored it and stepped boldly into the mist –

THUNK!

'Ow!'

– straight into a tree. As I rubbed my head, the mist and the tree and everything else dissolved, until there was nothing left.

Nothing. In front of me, Nothing. Behind me, Nothing. No Glenda, no flume, no road. I tried to look around, but around had gone. There was only Nothing.

I was afraid. Nothingness, true emptiness, the total not-there-ness of all things, is a freaky thing to experience. You can't see it – there's nothing there. You can't feel it, or hear it, or smell it. It's like stepping into a blank page. But blanker, and with no page.

'*Should've kept an eye on your brother, your brother, an eye, an eye . . .*'

'Ay-ay-ay!'

I swung round, staring into the emptiness that surrounded me. I knew that voice.

Then, from out of the Nothing came . . . *something*. An eye, another eye. A pair of familiar eyes, joined by a familiar grin, emerging cheekily through the void. The little Regret stopped squawking in my ear and flew off.

'Harley-arley-arley!' said the familiar mouth in its familiar voice. '*Vroom vroom VROOM!* That was proper clever what you done back there: finding an old codger when them Regrets was getting you down! Regrets *love* the oldies!'

Gradually, nose, eyebrows, ears and hands melted into view.

'Trouble is,' continued the boy, while arms, legs and all the rest of him materialised, 'you was about to regret letting your Regrets hop on the old woman, 'cos you didn't want to squash her. But if you *had* regretted it, they would've hopped back over to *you* – and the pair of you would've got stuck in a Regret-swapping-hopping loop! To me, to you, to me, to you . . .'

'A Regret-swapping-hopping?' I repeated mechanically. But I'd already lost interest in Glenda and the Regrets. I was too busy being gobsmacked by the return of my imaginary ex-friend.

Olly: the make-believe boy who'd ruined my life.

11

11:51 a.m. THURSDAY

22 hours and 9 minutes until Eternal Damnation

Oliver Polliver was eleven years old and always had been. When I'd first imagined him, three summers ago, I thought I was already too old for an imaginary friend. But there was no telling my mind that, so there he was.

It was the day after my parents gave me *The Big Book of Legendary Heroes and Mythical Monsters from All Myths and Legends All Over the World Ever* and I was feeling low. I guess I'd trusted my grandparents' stories, and now I didn't know what to rely on. Then Olly turned up and said I shouldn't believe stuff just because it was in a big book, or not believe stuff just because it wasn't. And that really boosted my confidence, even though I knew he was only saying it to be kind. So yeah, Olly was kind. Mainly though, he was just funnier and sillier and more *fun* than my other friends.

But, as the months went by, the fun turned into mischief. The mischief turned into trouble. And the trouble got serious. My parents despaired. My teachers despaired. *I* despaired. I'd become, in the words of Miss Stemper, my head teacher: 'The worst juvenile delinquent in the history of Kesmitherly!'

Because even though *Olly* was the one behind all the mischief-making, and messing about, and melting and mashing and mangling and meddling – I was the one who always got caught. Olly got away with it, every single time, because he was so good at sneaking and hiding and going unnoticed.

Then one day, just as things were getting really out of control, Olly disappeared. On Christmas Eve a year and a half ago, my imaginary friend abandoned me – even though he'd never existed in the first place! He vanished, leaving me to take the blame for everything.

The saddest thing was, if only people could've *met* Oliver Polliver, everything would've been fine. They'd have thought he was cheeky and silly and funny, and we'd have never got in *serious* trouble. Being best friends with a REAL Olly would've been amazing!

But no one ever did meet him because he didn't exist.

He was just inside my head.

And now here he was again, beaming at me out of the void. He was literally all I could see. Just Olly, and Nothing.

But why? Why was he here? Why had my crazy mind conjured him up now, down here, when I had so much other crazy stuff to deal with?

'To be honest, Harley-arley-arley,' said Olly, leaning against Nothing and casually spinning some professional moves with his yo-yo, 'I was proper shocked to hear you'd passed through. You was the *last* person I expected to die young. You was always so *sensible* when I wanted us to do bonkers dangerous stuff. But I was well pleased to be chosen as your Guide.'

'*You're* my Guide?'

'Oliver Polliver at your service, madam!'

He bowed, saluted, and curtseyed for good measure.

'Quality, ain't it?' he said, his yo-yo spinning nonchalantly through the emptiness. 'Me as your personal Guide to the Back of Beyond. Everyone's got their special someone – usually it's your mum or your dog. You got *me*! Oy! Oy!'

'Why you?' I couldn't believe it! 'Of all the *real* dead people or animals – why *you*?'

'You're sort of hurting my feelings now, Harley-arley-arley. You could at least *pretend* to be pleased to see me.'

'Yeah, sorry,' I said. 'It just seems quite an important job for an imaginary person. I guess I assumed my Guide would be someone . . . real.'

'Yeah, well . . . Listen, Harley-arley-arley – *vroom vroom VROOM!* – I got something I need to tell you,' said Olly, shuffling about awkwardly. 'Thing is, I ain't just a salt-of-the-earth wheeler-dealer geezer.' He spun the yo-yo round his head – a move he called the Wicked Windmill – and looked at me.

'I'm dead.'

'Okay,' I said. 'And what difference does that make, seeing as you're not real?'

'No, I *am* real. I'm just dead.'

He continued to stare and spin, waiting for this massive shock to sink in. It didn't sink in though, because I didn't believe him. He was imaginary, so I didn't have to.

'You think I'm in your head,' Olly went on, 'but I'm not. I'm dead. I've been dead since 1989.'

I hesitated. Olly was probably talking rubbish, like usual. Then again, he'd always been different. I'd just assumed that's what imaginary friends were like. But looking at him now, I wondered if there was more to it – the white plimsolls, the luminous socks, the turquoise shell suit. There was something . . . *historic* about the whole look.

My mind drifted back to a cold, drizzly night, a year and a half earlier. I was lying awake, staring at the lonely shadow cast by the stocking at the end of my bed, when suddenly, I heard a noise outside. A ghostly swoosh, a rattle and a clatter.

Could it be? Could it really be . . .? Father Christmas! Santa Claus! Saint Nick!

I rushed to the window and threw up the sash, like a girl in a Victorian poem. But it wasn't Santa.

That morning was the last time I'd seen Olly. He'd been going on and on at me to put the half-defrosted turkey in Mum and Dad's bed – 'It'll be epic laughs!' – and I got fed up with it all. I stormed off and locked myself in the bathroom, and I told Harley in the mirror that she was too old for an imaginary friend and it was time for him to go.

Then he went. No goodbye, no apology. He just abandoned me. Popped out of my head and stopped existing. Left me to deal with the consequences of being the worst juvenile delinquent in the history of Kesmitherly.

I figured I must've shaken him out of my brain. Later that night, I wondered if I'd shaken all the other fun stuff out too, when it turned out the noise outside my window wasn't the clatter of reindeer hooves. It was just a rusty old coach. A great big, shimmering . . . *ghostly* coach.

Oh.

That's where I'd seen it before!

'BK picked you up that night,' I said.

Olly shrugged. 'Seemed like I'd outstayed my welcome after them things you said.'

'You were *listening*?'

'Yeah, well. It was clear you didn't want me around. So I got a lift to the caravan and plopped down through your grandparents' bog.'

'So you were *dead*, the whole time I knew you?' I said. 'You were a ghost?'

'Woo-oo-oo-oooo!' said Olly.

'Everyone thought you didn't exist, but you were *real*?'

'Yeah! They just couldn't see me. That's why they all thought you was bonkers! Oy! Oy!'

'But *I* could see you,' I said.

'Well, yeah. Visionaries could see me, obviously,' said Olly. 'The whole thing was your grandparents' idea. Before I met you, I'd already been a Restless Soul for more than thirty years, wandering about as a mischievous ghostie, spooking people for laughs – *BOO!* Ha ha! I'd been dead since 1989. But I still wasn't ready to come *down here,* even though I was long overdue. Then old Gran and that lot came up with their scheme. They thought it'd be good for you to spend some time with a Restless Soul so you could get used to it, ready for your Visionary Duties. Problem was, your mum and dad wouldn't have approved of a dead friend. So I snuck about, kept out of their way, and pretended you'd imagined me.'

'My grandparents made you be my fake-imaginary-actually-dead-secret-friend?' I said.

'They didn't *make* me. They *asked* me. And I said, why not? And I didn't regret it! You was my funniest favouritest mate what I ever had – alive *or* dead! And it was proper hilarious, because everyone thought I was just in your head. They thought you was doing all them outrageous things by yourself!'

Olly was laughing like crazy.

'It's not funny!' I said. 'It ruined my life! I had to have counselling! The Bishop of Risborough booked me in for an exorcism!'

'Yeah, it got a bit out of hand. Sorry about that. But you liked it at the time, Harley-arley-arley! And as soon as you was over it, I upped and left. Drank the *Special Tea,* popped in the Portal, and *KERPOW!* – I'm proper dead. Just like you.'

12

12:02 p.m. THURSDAY

21 hours and 58 minutes
until Eternal Damnation

'So now that we've got all that out the way,' said Olly, 'I better kick off this Guide thing again more proper like.'

'Okay, whatever,' I said, willing to play along if it meant we could get out of this Nothingness and closer to finding Malcolm.

'Welcome to *Beyond*, Miss Lenton!' said Olly, with a bow and a salute and a curtsey. 'My name is Oliver, and I'm your official Guide. Please step this way.'

Olly took my hand and led me through the emptiness.

'How do you know where you're going?' I asked as he

moved confidently through the Nothingness.

'Been through here before, ain't I? With my old man.'

'Your dad?'

Olly went quiet for a moment, then changed the subject. 'So how did you die so young, then?'

'Actually, I'm not de—'

I stopped myself. It suddenly occurred to me that Olly mustn't know my real reason for being here. Right now, he thought I was just an ordinary dead person, and I wanted it to stay that way. If Olly knew about my mission to rescue Malcolm, he'd get way too excited, and start coming up with schemes and plans and just generally try to get *involved*.

'I'm not de— discussing it,' I said. 'You know, it's still quite upsetting.'

'Fair enough,' said Olly, casually propelling his yo-yo into a Revolutionary Roundabout.

And now I really wanted to know how *he'd* died, and why he didn't want to talk about his dad. But I didn't ask, figuring it'd be safer to avoid the subject. It was usually better not to talk about things like that.

We walked on in silence.

'See this Nothingness?' said Olly, who could only do silence for a few seconds. '*This* is why you need a Guide to get you through to the Back of Beyond. A Guide you can trust.'

'Who says I trust you?' I said.

'Well, I'm here, ain't I? And these crocodiles haven't bitten your legs off, and you haven't fallen into that chasm over there, and you haven't burnt your b—'

'Yeah, all right, I get it,' I said. 'You're pretending there's a load of scary stuff around so you can hold my hand.'

'No, I ain't! Let go if you don't believe me – see if I care!'

I let go.

'There's a pit of snakes here. I can guide you round it.'

'I'll take my chances.'

'Fair enough, Harley-arley-arley! *Vroom vroom VROOOOM!*'

The *vroom vroom VROOM!* thing was getting kind of annoying. I guess I used to find it funny, back when Olly was older than me. It was meant to be the noise of the famously big motorbike I'm named after. Apparently, when they were younger, Mum and Dad used to dream of riding a Harley across the desert. Then they decided that owning a motorbike would be too expensive and too dangerous and would make them too interesting. So as a compromise, they'd named their daughter after the motorbike they couldn't have. Fortunately, by the time their second child was born, eleven years later, they'd matured enough to give him a human name.

I stomped through the Nothingness, thinking about the Bad Times. All those "discussions" in Miss Stemper's office, when everyone thought I was blaming my bad behaviour on a completely made-up imaginary friend – and it always felt unfair because Olly seemed so *real* to me. And even though I kept telling myself he *couldn't* be real, I could never shake the question of why *my brain* would invent a friend who was so . . . Olly-ish? And now it made sense. I hadn't created him from the depths of my subconscious mind at all. He was just a real dead boy my grandparents wanted me to hang out with. You know, to prepare me for an unpaid job serving tea to other dead people.

'Fancy a game of I-Spy?' Olly asked. 'Ha ha ha! Joking! 'Cos there's *nothing*, see? So we couldn't. Not far to the main road now.'

'The Road to Nowhere?'

'No, the Road to the Back of Beyond. The Road to Nowhere don't go nowhere. We done that bit. Next, we go to the Back of Beyond.'

Olly rambled on. He loved being a Guide.

'All of this is *Beyond*, see. Not just this Nothingness – the whole lot. It's *beyond* life as we knew it *before*. That's why they call it *Beyond*. The bit before, we generally call *Before* – that's what you'd probably call Life. But the thing about *Beyond* is you've got to get to the very *back* of it for the good stuff. The front of *Beyond* ain't worth bothering with – as you can see. Or rather, as you *can't* see. Aha! Here we are: the Road to the Back of Beyond!'

Olly flung his arms wide as the Nothingness dissolved,

and a road melted into view beneath our feet. This road stretched ahead of us for miles and miles, across a flat, empty landscape, until it disappeared into far distant hills.

'Is there a bus?' I asked.

'There's something better than a bus!' Olly replied.

I looked around, half expecting a fake unicorn, but hoping for a magic carpet or a flagon of Mega-Fast Sprinting Potion –

'There's a song!' Olly announced. 'A cheery song to keep our spirits up!'

My heart sank. Olly always did a "cheery song" at the worst possible moments – like all those times outside Miss Stemper's office, waiting to be told off for some prank *he'd* made me do. I'd be sitting there quietly, and he'd start singing and prancing about, trying really hard to make me laugh . . . and then, just as Miss Stemper opened her door, I'd giggle at his stupid face and get into even more trouble.

Still, there was no point trying to stop him. You couldn't stop Olly.

> *'Oy! Oy! Oy! Bish bash bosh!*
> *Ding dong dang! Gilly gilly gosh!*
> *We're going to the back to the back to the back*
> *We're off to the Back of Beyond! OY!'*

'Don't worry,' he said, 'there's only one verse – it just

repeats. You'll pick it up after a few goes. Come on, get your knees up! Don't dawdle!'

He bounced on, with a knock-kneed, elbow-jutting dance.

'Oy! Oy! Oy! Bish bash bosh . . .'

After forty verses, I realised I had to get rid of him. Olly was a distraction, like he always had been. The Dead-Not-Imaginary news might've changed everything about my past, but it didn't affect the present. He needed to go, so that I could focus on finding Malcolm and getting Back to Life. Besides, what with BK's soulful vocals on the heath this morning, there was just too much singing. My Epic Quest into the Land of the Dead was beginning to feel like a low-budget musical.

I sped up.

'You got somewhere you need to be?' Olly asked.

'No, I . . . No, of course not.'

I slowed down again. Whatever happened, I mustn't let Olly guess what I was up to. If he had any idea I was secretly still alive and on a perilous rescue mission, he'd want to help – and then I'd *never* get rid of him. Best thing I could do right now was to act like a normal dead person, and not arouse suspicion. Eventually, he'd get bored and leave me alone.

'Fancy an ice cream?' he asked as we passed a roadside kiosk.

'Erm,' I said.

Obviously I wanted an ice cream. And saying yes to an ice cream was a perfect way to prove I was normal and boring and not on a quest. But I *was* on a quest, and having an ice cream on a quest felt a bit cheeky – like watching YouTube when you're meant to be doing your homework. On the other hand, we'd been walking for *ages.* Maybe I deserved a treat?

'Two Cornettos, please!' said Olly, leaning casually on the counter.

'There you go,' said the kiosk man. 'That'll be twenty minutes, please.'

'Pardon?' I said.

'Ten-minute chat for each ice cream, that's twenty minutes of conversation in total,' he explained.

'A twenty-minute conversation?' I clarified.

'Yep.'

'Can I just pay with money instead?'

'Nope.'

'But I haven't *got* twenty minutes! Here, have it back.'

'Can't take that back. You've torn the wrapper.'

'Come on, Harley-arley-arley – it's only twenty minutes,' said Olly, relaxing on a beige verge. 'What's the panic anyway? No point rushing through Eternity.'

I couldn't believe it. *Twenty minutes!* The afterlife was turning out to be a frustratingly laid-back place for someone in a hurry. These chilled-out dead people were really stressing me out.

'Have you heard the latest?' asked the kiosk man, kicking off the chat that was happening whether I liked it or not.

'What latest?' I asked impatiently.

'About the new Legendary Hero,' said the kiosk man.

I perked up, intrigued by his choice of topic. 'What do you mean?'

'He's talking about Idolicles,' said Olly, lying back and staring lazily at the clouds. 'But he ain't exactly new.'

'No, not him,' interrupted the kiosk man. 'There's an even newer one than Idolicles.'

Olly sat up. 'Another one? Already?'

'Yep,' said the kiosk man. 'There was a prophecy on Tuesday . . .'

'Oh, I heard *that*,' said Olly, lying back down. 'But you can't believe everything you hear from them soothsayers. They make most of it up.'

'Well, not this time. Apparently, this new Hero has *arrived*,' announced the kiosk man.

Olly sat up again. 'Seriously? Arrived already? A new Legendary Hero? A fresh one?'

'Seriously,' confirmed the kiosk man. 'A new Legendary Hero. Here, today – to save the innocent and bring HOPE to us all!'

13

1:06 p.m. THURSDAY

20 hours and 54 minutes
until Eternal Damnation

Olly was so excited about the kiosk man's news, he got his yo-yo out and did a Hot Swinging Jeffrey between his legs. 'I can't *believe* there's a fresh Legendary Hero already!'

'Yep,' said the kiosk man. 'Landed *Beyond* earlier today. And the Welcoming Committee has already organised a Heroic Picnic for this afternoon.'

'Crikey wowser!' said Olly. 'It's only been a week since Idolicles!'

'I know! They're like buses, these Legendary Heroes – you wait around for centuries, then two come along at once!'

Olly and the kiosk man laughed like a pack of hyenas with a whoopee cushion.

'I don't get it,' I said.

My dead friend turned to me with his serious joke-explaining face. 'You know when you're at the bus stop –'

'No, I get *that*,' I said. 'But I don't get why you're talking about Legendary Heroes like they're real. I don't get how a *Legendary* Hero *can* be real.'

'Didn't you read the Information Brochure?' asked the kiosk man.

'Legendary Heroes are Living Visionaries who come *Beyond* on purpose,' Olly explained, slipping back into Guide mode. 'Usually they come down to rescue an Innocent Living Soul who's accidentally travelled here *before their time.* We had a geezer last week – Idolicles – come down to rescue his wife. Apparently, she was a famous gymnast who died too soon, doing Cartwheels for Charity down the motorway. The internet got sad because she was famously beautiful, so her Hero husband came to fetch her back up.'

'But that's old news,' interrupted the kiosk man. 'Today we got a *new* Legendary Hero, turned up this morning.'

'So you're talking about a real live Legendary Hero who's come down here to rescue someone?' I said.

'Yeah!' said Olly. 'Hey, we should go to the Welcoming Picnic! Check this new Hero out, live on stage in the Happy Meadow! What d'you reckon, Harley-arley-arley?'

Well, I was still getting used to having a *real* imaginary friend and meeting a bunch of *real* dead people. And now I was being invited to see a real live Legendary Hero who'd just arrived from *Before* to rescue an Innocent Living Soul.

But hold on a minute . . . this was perfect! A *real* Hero was exactly what I needed! If they were down here rescuing someone already, they might as well help me rescue my brother at the same time. I could picture it now: a noble warrior, leaping fearlessly across a fiery chasm with me and Malcolm clinging on . . .

'Picnic sounds great!' I said.

'Don't get your hopes up, though,' said the kiosk man, wiping the counter with a damp cloth. 'Idolicles was a *Classic* Legendary Hero, like back in the day. All brave and strong and decisive. But a lot of these *Modern* Legendary Heroes aren't like that at all. To put it frankly, they're wimps! Always going on about feelings and empathy and tolerance.'

Olly shook his head and sighed. 'They don't make 'em like they used to!'

'Half of them run out of time on the Path of Heroes!'

'Or can't handle the Twelve Tasks!'

'Or get torn to pieces by a spooky monster!'

'Or fall *Beneath*!'

'And *then* get torn to pieces!'

'Okay, okay,' I interrupted. 'Slow down a minute, one thing at a time.'

I figured I should make the most of this conversation, since I apparently owed it anyway. I might as well find out as much as I could about what lay ahead. After all, this new Legendary Hero might turn out to be a Modern Wimp instead of a Classic Legend like Idolly-whatnot – so I'd better be ready to step up, just in case.

'So this Path of Heroes,' I said. 'What's it like?'

'The Path of Heroes is horrific and terrifying and full of creepy monsters and that sort of thing!' said the kiosk man, waving his arms in a spooky-tentacle sort of way.

'It's what the Legendary Hero goes along,' said Olly, 'before passing through the Fire Exit and Back to Life. Unless it all goes wrong, in which case they're *TRAPPED FOREVER IN ETERNAL DAMNATION*!'

'With all the creepy monsters and that sort of thing!' repeated the kiosk man, waggling his tentacles again.

'And why might they get trapped forever?' I asked.

'Either 'cos they're too slow, or 'cos they fail the Twelve Tasks.'

'Okay,' I said. 'And these Twelve Tasks. Are they . . . tricky?'

The kiosk man slapped his damp cloth on the counter and leaned forward, knocking his plastic spoons over. 'The Twelve Tasks aren't tricky,' he whispered. 'They're *impossible*!'

I looked at my Cornetto. I'd reached the last bite – the best bite – the bite that remains when it's been munched down into a tiny cone full of chocolate, like a mini ice cream for a baby monkey in an ice-cream testing laboratory. Usually, I *loved* arriving at that tiny crunchy mini cone. But I'd suddenly lost my appetite.

'Impossible?' I gulped.

'It's not impossible,' said Olly. '*Some* Legendary Heroes have done it.'

'*Some* have, yes,' said the kiosk man. 'Like Idolicles, for example – I bet he did.'

'So it's *not* impossible?' I clarified.

'Not *literally* impossible, I suppose. But it's very . . . tricky.'

'It's things like racing the Swift-Footed Gazellopuss – to the death,' said Olly. 'Tickling the Venomous Piranhagator – to the death. Arm-wrestling the Many-Limbed Optimugoon . . .'

'To the death!' said the kiosk man.

'Yeah,' said Olly. 'Always to the death.'

'The Swift-Footed Gazellopuss?' I said. 'The Many-Limbed Optimugoon? But *they're* not real. They're definitely not real.'

'Bet you wouldn't say that if one bit your head off,' said the kiosk man.

'But the Many-Limbed Optimugoon . . .' Then I stopped

talking because I realised my recent track record on what was real or not real was just hopeless. For a moment, I'd been certain these monsters weren't real – not only because they were monsters and sounded made-up, but also because these particular monsters were from my grandparents' totally fake, no-one-else-has-ever-heard-of-them myths.

But there was another possibility. My grandparents' stories had always *felt* real. What if they were? Not real like the stories in *The Big Book of Legendary Heroes and Mythical Monsters from All Myths and Legends All Over the World Ever*, but *really* real? What if *their* Legendary Heroes and Mythical Monsters actually existed? What if their stories had *actually happened?* And what if Nana's landscape of mist and shadow was the Path of Heroes?

'This time limit you mentioned,' I said. 'I'm guessing it might be something like twenty-four hours . . .?'

'The alignment of the celestial spheres –' the kiosk man began.

'Is it twenty-four hours?' I snapped.

'Yep, more or less,' said the kiosk man, picking up his plastic spoons and putting them in their pot.

Twenty-four hours! Just like in the stories!

'But even if the Legendary Hero *doesn't* run out of time,' said the kiosk man, 'and *doesn't* get eaten by a monster, and *doesn't* fail the Twelve Tasks . . . there's always the risk of falling *BENEATH.'*

'What's *Beneath*?' I asked.

'I'm not quite sure, to be honest. But it's worse than the Many-Limbed Optimugoon, so it must be very nasty.'

I still couldn't get my head round the idea that these totally weird but totally scary monsters might be real. As it happened, the Many-Limbed Optimugoon was one of my personal favourite deadly mythical beasts – I loved the way Pops flailed about, snapping and snarling as he described its many limbs in intricate, terrifying detail. But I liked it from the safety of a sleeping bag in a caravan; I didn't want to meet one on a spooky path.

'Erm, just to clarify,' I said, 'is passing along the Path of Heroes definitely the only way out? Are you sure there's not another, more sensible route Back to Life? A secret passageway, perhaps? Or maybe you could sneak out the entrance?'

'No secret passages,' said the kiosk man. 'And the entrance is a downpipe. Can't go up it.'

'Basic plumbing,' added Olly, tucking his thumbs knowledgeably into his belt.

'Path of Heroes, Twelve Tasks, terrifying beasts, Fire Exit.' The kiosk man leaned over his counter. 'It's the only way,' he whispered. 'And it's *impossible*!'

'*Impossible* like last time you said *impossible*?' I asked. 'As in "not impossible"?'

'Yep,' he admitted, placing the final spoon in his spoon-pot. 'It is *very tricky*, though. Let me put it another way. In the last ten thousand years, only a handful of Legendary Heroes have successfully come down here, rescued someone from Death, and returned to Life. Three arms and a legful have failed. So realistically, the chances of any Hero making it out are a million to one.'

'A million to one?' I yelped.

The kiosk man looked unsure. 'A hundred to one?' he said, counting his fingers. 'Look, I don't know the exact numbers, but the point is, there's more stories about Heroes *failing* than *succeeding*.'

'Stories,' I said. 'Are you telling me all your information is based on *stories*?'

'What else is there?' said the kiosk man. 'Did you see the football last night?'

'Oh no – no, no, no,' I said. 'Don't go changing the subject. I'm not done with our last conversation. When you say *stories*, do you mean the stories told by successful Heroes?'

'No, not really,' said Olly. 'Once they're back down –

after they've died normally – True Legendary Heroes don't really talk about their time on the Path of Heroes. They just pop by to collect their medals, then sail up the River Betwixt to those private islands off the Luxury Coast. That's like the VIP section of the Back of Beyond. We don't hear much from them after that.'

'So if it's not from the Heroes themselves, where do these monster-battling stories come from?' I asked.

The kiosk man shrugged. 'It's just stuff people know. I mean, there is a lot of *paintings* of Heroes fighting monsters. And there is a lot of *movies* with Heroes fighting monsters.'

'Yeah,' said Olly. 'But in the movies, the Heroes and monsters are just actors in Hero and monster costumes. And the costumes are based on the paintings. And the artists who done the paintings ain't actually *seen* any of it, obviously, 'cos they're too busy painting.'

'Okay, okay, never mind,' I said, aware that time was ticking on.

I stared down the Road to the Back of Beyond and took a deep breath. If there was a chance of Real Mythical Monsters, I'd be needing a Real Legendary Hero. And, as luck would have it, there was one turning up at a special picnic this afternoon.

'Soothsayer reckons it'll rain later,' said the kiosk man, scrabbling about for two ice-cream's worth of conversation.

'Okay, bye,' I said, and set off.

'Hey! That's only twelve minutes!' he shouted.

'My friend'll pay the rest!' I shouted back.

I marched on, my eyes fixed on the road ahead.

It was Picnic Time.

An hour later, the road ended at the foot of the underworld's second tallest escalator. I knew it was the underworld's second tallest escalator because of the sign next to it – an enormous, multicoloured, sparkly, glittery, luminous, twirling, brightly flashing sign that said:

TRAVEL IN STYLE AND COMFORT

ON THE UNDERWORLD'S SECOND TALLEST ESCALATOR!

As I approached, I noticed a handwritten note Blu-tacked to the bottom step:

OUT OF ORDER

Sorry for ~~inconvin~~ ~~inconvei~~ it being broken

Forty minutes later, at the top, I stopped to catch my breath.

I stared at the awesome valley below.

This was the Back of Beyond.

And everyone who had ever been, was there.

PART THREE

THE BACK OF BEYOND

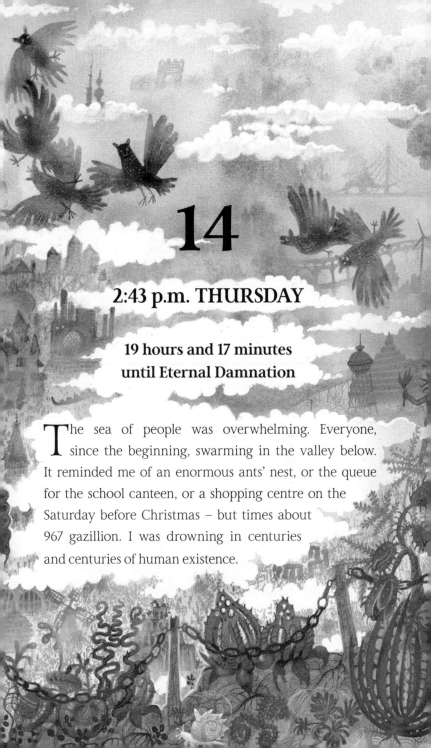

14

2:43 p.m. THURSDAY

19 hours and 17 minutes until Eternal Damnation

The sea of people was overwhelming. Everyone, since the beginning, swarming in the valley below. It reminded me of an enormous ants' nest, or the queue for the school canteen, or a shopping centre on the Saturday before Christmas – but times about 967 gazillion. I was drowning in centuries and centuries of human existence.

PHLOOOMP!

I stared at the endless crowds of dead people. It was hopeless. I'd never find Malcolm among that lot.

PHLOOOMP! PHLOOOMP!

This was a whole new level of letting my parents down. In a pathetic attempt to rescue their favourite child from Death, I'd gone and lost their second favourite child too.

PHLOOOMP! PHLOOOMP! PHLOOOMP! PHLOOOMP!

Bristly blobs leapt on to my back and squelched on to my legs. They kept coming, clinging on with their oily tentacles until the weight of them crushed me to the ground, and I was completely swamped.

My phone buzzed. Slowly, I slid my arm through the slimy gaps between Regrets and reached into my rucksack. Then I slid my arm back through the squelchy crevices and held the phone in front of my face. The screen shone brightly in the darkness of my blubbery coffin.

> Hi Harley. how r u? Should we join u in the caravan 2nite with a takeaway? A treat 4 everyone 2 celebrate the new boiler! Would u like that? MUM xxx

I pictured Mum and Dad arriving at the caravan to discover their entire family had disappeared, while I lay here, uselessly buried in the Back of Beyond. It was awful, but it gave me an idea.

> Hi Mum. Me and Maccy BURIED IN SAND on Frimpton beach! So much fun!!!! But long and tiring day out so no takeaway tonight, thanks. See you in the morning. H xxx

> OK. Bet it's busy down there 2day ;)
> Give our love 2 everyone. & Be careful xxx

Another pair of Regrets piled on as they sensed how lying to Mum made me feel. This is it, I thought. This is how it ends. Not slain by a terrible monster on the Path of Heroes – but here, on a cold hilltop, crushed for eternity beneath a mound of wriggly blobs.

'Too many Regrets!' I moaned to nobody.

'These ain't all Regrets,' said Olly, squatting down in front of me and scooping a tentacle out of my eye.

Oh great. And now my Official Guide to the Back of Beyond was here, to see how brilliantly I was coping without him.

'Some of these are Doubts,' he explained. 'Very similar, but a Doubt's hairier than a Regret. Shake?'

'That makes it worse!' I whined. 'I've done this before, remember.'

'No, not *shake*. "Shake?" As in, "Would you like one?" I brung it for you from the kiosk.'

He shoved a milkshake in my face.

'Oh. Thanks.' As I slurped through the straw, a couple of Doubts dissolved, and a medium-sized Regret hopped off my shoulders towards some other poor Soul.

'How does anyone ever find *anyone* in this place?' I groaned.

'Don't worry about that lot. It looks hectic at first, but everyone finds each other eventually. I found you, didn't I?'

'But how did they all get here?' I asked. 'There wasn't even a queue for the flume!'

'Well, for starters,' said Olly, 'there's thousands of Portals and thousands of flumes – but only a teensy tiny portion come through like that anyway. Most Dead Souls just sort of wake up here one day. Heart attack – *ouch!* – Back of Beyond. Hit by a bus – *splat!* – Back of Beyond. Fallen out a window whilst ironing a curtain (should've taken it down, mate!) – *crumph!* – Back of Beyond. Eaten by a bear –'

'Okay, I get the idea.'

'It's just *Restless* Souls that come through a Portal. And Heroes. Ready?'

'For what?'

'Hold on tight!'

And then Olly did something even more annoying and painful than his *bish bash bosh* song; he grabbed my arms and dragged me along the ground.

'Hey! What're you doing?' I yelled.

'Doubts and Regrets,' Olly explained, as he puffed and heaved, 'are banned . . . in the Back . . . of Beyond. Just need to get you . . . into the zone . . . and this lot will disappear.'

As he hauled me over the stony ground, I felt claws and suction pads tightening their grip. The blobby parasites crushed me, the rocky terrain bruised me, and Olly nearly pulled my arms off. This was a classic example of why I didn't like being *helped*.

'The Back of Beyond,' Olly continued breathlessly, 'is a Doubts and Regrets Free Zone. From just over here . . . all the way to the River Betwixt. It's the rules.'

Sure enough, at the top of the down escalator, the Doubts and Regrets vanished. I sat up to examine my wounds.

'Bet that feels better,' said Olly, sitting beside me.

It did feel better, despite the bruises. But I didn't want to encourage him, so I just mumbled a quiet sort of *thanks* noise and stood up to leave. This Olly friendliness was getting out of hand, and I knew from experience it could only lead to trouble and betrayal and getting distracted – and I couldn't risk any of that in the middle of a Rescue Mission from Death.

*

At the bottom of the escalator, we joined a merry crowd of dead people strolling along with hampers and blankets. At a guess, there were about eight bazillion of them. It felt like the whole world was heading towards the Heroic Picnic. Then we arrived at the Happy Meadow, and I realised the whole world was already there. I started counting picnickers and reached about fifty squillion before I gave up.

'Are all these people here to see the Hero?' I asked, staring in disbelief.

'Well . . . yes and no,' said Olly. 'A Hero Welcoming is a bit like a royal wedding. People pretend to be interested, but really it's just an excuse to have a day off and eat sausage rolls. Most of this lot are only here for the free concert.'

We zigzagged across the meadow, between rugs and sandwiches and deckchairs and lemonade. Some groups of picnickers were huge, with hundreds of blankets connected into a patchwork village; others were very small.

'As you can see,' said Olly, 'the Dead stick to their own.' As we strolled on, he pointed out some of the picnicking cliques. 'You see that lot – they all fell off ladders. That lot over there – swallowed by hippos. This lot – choked on fishbones . . .'

I looked more closely at the death clans and realised I could guess what some of the others might be. To my left, a jolly group of lawnmower victims were making each other giggle. To my right, a cheerful bunch of drowned people were sharing a box of doughnuts. Behind me, a happy troupe of over-ambitious acrobats was playing Twister. We passed a group of men with flattened bowler hats. 'They've been here a while,' Olly whispered. 'People don't get squashed by pianos much any more.'

'But what about family?' I blurted out, afraid that Malcolm might've got separated from Nana.

'Family's family,' Olly reassured me. 'Can't escape your family. And most families have different death origins, so it all gets mixed up in the end.'

It was a relief to think that Malcolm and Nana would've probably met up with my other grandparents. And they'd be easier to spot in a group – if they were even here. I scanned the endless swarm of picnickers, anxiously aware of the minutes ticking away.

'Olly! Olly! Olly!' shouted a group of kids, charging towards us across the meadow.

'Oy! Oy! Oy!' shouted Olly in response.

'Olly! Olly! Olly!' they shouted again, slaloming wildly between picnickers.

'Oy! Oy! Oy!' shouted Olly.

Olly's friends ran up to us, bouncing about madly like wallabies at a silent disco. In fact, they were wriggling and rolling and weaving so much, it took me a while to realise

there were only three of them. Watching them was like trying to keep up with a street magician doing the three-cup trick.

'What's up?' said the foot-tapping jittery girl.

'How's it going?' said the boy who was shaking so fast he kept going out of focus.

'Where you been?' said the boy who lurched about looking permanently surprised.

'Hello, lads,' said Olly. 'This is my mate, Harley-arley-arley – vroom *vroom VROOM!* – you know, from *Before.*'

'Hello, Harley!' said the blurry boy, shaking my hand. 'I'm Sparky.'

'Good to meet you!' said the jumpy girl. 'I'm Elektra!'

'Hey!' said the surprised boy. 'I'm Frazzle.'

'Hi,' I said.

'Bet you're wondering what happened to us!' said Olly.

'Erm,' I said, wondering if I could check the time on my phone without anyone noticing.

'We were all electrocuted,' Elektra explained, 'whilst climbing an electricity pylon to fetch a Frisbee.'

'Not the same Frisbee!' said Frazzle, laughing.

'No. Different Frisbees, different pylons – different places, different times,' said Sparky. 'We didn't know each other *Before*.'

'And all that high voltage is why we're so full of energy!' said Olly, whipping out his yo-yo and spinning a Diamond Propeller which the others dived through like squirrels on sherbet.

'How did you die, Harley?' asked Elektra, with a friendly smile.

'Oh, I, er, didn't eat my vegetables,' I lied. 'Anyway, I've got to go and find . . . someone.'

I decided to leave my phone in my bag. Whatever time it was, it certainly wasn't meeting-new-people time. Sure, Olly's high-voltage friends were high-voltage friendly – but this was classic Olly. I needed to avoid distractions and focus on finding Malcolm, not get tempted away from my mission by Crazy Fun Times! Soon enough the batteries would run down on Crazy Fun Times, like they always did. And then then there'd be Trouble, and then there'd be Bad Times – and down here, Bad Times were going to be *really* bad, like Eternal Damnation bad.

'Who you gotta find?' asked Olly.

'Erm, Nana,' I said. I was running out of lies, and I figured Olly could know a little bit of truth without guessing the rest. Besides, visiting an elderly relative seemed like the perfect excuse to get away.

'Nana's *dead*? That's brilliant! I ain't seen her in yonks!' Olly turned to his friends. 'You gotta meet Harley's Nana – she's a total legend!'

'We'll help you find her!' said Elektra.

'No,' I said, too quickly.

Elektra looked deflated. All four of them drooped, like puppies who've been denied a treat. This was so typical. Meeting new people always led to this kind of awkwardness.

'Okay – yes, then. You can come and meet her,' I said. Their faces lit up and they started bouncing again, wagging their imaginary tails. 'I'll meet you back here in five minutes. I'm just going to the loo.'

I left the Pylon Kids listening to Olly's stories about my "epic Nana" and headed off towards the portaloos.

But as soon as they weren't looking, I dived to the ground and commando-crawled past the toilets, creeping behind picnickers until I was out of sight. I felt bad about sneaking off, but I was on a mission. I didn't have time for all this *friends* stuff.

15

3:24 p.m. THURSDAY

18 hours and 36 minutes
until Eternal Damnation

I jogged across the meadow towards the main stage by the banks of the River Betwixt. My plan was to rush the stage and beg the Legendary Hero for help while everyone was watching. I figured it'd be hard for them to say no in front of a bazillion people.

As I got nearer, I watched the enormous screens on either side of the stage. They were showing old movie clips of Legendary Heroes battling Mythical Monsters. And yes, these scenes really did seem to be monster-battling moments from my grandparents' stories! Here was Craemog the Intrepid, fearlessly slaying the slippery

Mega-Worm; here was Vileeda the Valiant, courageously wrestling the Razor-Elbowed Glockenpard; here was Hallyria the Unrelenting, bravely being bitten and stung by a swarm of sabre-toothed wasps. As far as people down here were concerned, my grandparents' fake myths were real history!

And the crowd was loving it. As they watched, they oohed and aahed, and held up homemade banners which said things like:

Occasionally, the screens cut away from the movie scenes to a live feed of the crowd watching itself. One of the zillions of drones buzzing over the meadow would zoom in on a group of picnickers, and when they saw themselves on the big screens, they'd cheer and wave and point at themselves, cheering and waving and pointing at themselves.

'The arrival of the prophesied Legendary Hero will be followed LIVE, throughout the afternoon!' announced the host onstage, his voice blasting from a thousand speakers. 'As officials from the Hero Welcoming Committee finalise their preparations, we could hardly hope for more perfect weather on this historic day – here, in the beautiful Happy Meadow! Behind me, on the other side of the River Betwixt, we see a rather different picture. As always, the far shore is shrouded in terrifying darkness! And somewhere in that miserable fog is the Gateway to the Path of Heroes – the only route Back to Life for Living Visionaries who have travelled *Beyond*!'

As I jogged towards the stage, I looked at the miserable fog across the river and wished I was back in Kesmitherly.

'And of course, we're all fervently hoping that today's prophesied Hero will be as brave and strong as last week's,' continued the commentator. 'Ah, Noble Idolicles! Idolicles the Champion! So brave, so strong, so magnificent! And who could forget his beautiful wife, the fair Lovelia! Brought down to us too soon, while cartwheeling along the motorway for charity . . . Such a tragedy. But by *now*, of course, noble Idolicles will have slain the monsters, completed the Tasks, and rescued her!

Ah, what an Epic Tale his brave struggles will make! If only it were possible to witness his courageous deeds as they happened. But alas, none of us can see into the present; we must patiently await the legends. For now, let us hope that today's prophesied Hero will be another *True Hero* – like Brave Idolicles and the Heroes of Old!'

For a moment, I panicked. I knew the odds were against today's Hero being like Brave Idolicles, but I didn't have a Plan B. What if this new Hero didn't *want* to help me rescue Malcolm? What if they weren't brave or strong enough to bother trying? If only Malcolm had been swept into the Land of the Dead last week, when Noble Idolicles had been passing through.

I didn't get to panic about this for long, however, because a moment later I had to stop and panic about something else. A huge metal fence stood between me and the stage. I couldn't even *reach* the Hero! It was one of those massive temporary fences they use for festivals, where each panel slots together. I tried to push it and lift it, but it wouldn't budge.

Stepping back, I noticed a sign near the top.

PRIVATE PICNIC ZONE

FRIENDS AND FAMILY OF

PROPHESIED HERO <u>ONLY</u>

I was about to try climbing it, when someone yelled, 'Look, the Legendary Hero's arrived! Over there!'

People went crazy, jostling each other to try and spot the Legendary Hero, as the news spread through the crowd. Within a minute, a million voices were wondering where their Hero was.

'I can now confirm the rumours,' announced the commentator over the hubbub. 'The Legendary Hero has, indeed, arrived in the Happy Meadow! We're hoping to bring you live footage of this historic figure, any minute now . . .'

Excitement gave way to mayhem. Mayhem gave way to pandemonium. Picnickers pushed and shoved to see over the heads of others, trampling samosas and sausages and sushi in their desperation.

Then, on the other side of the fence, amongst the enormous Family of the Prophesied Hero, I spotted four familiar old people and a small child playing with a cat I used to know.

'Maccy!' I yelled. 'Grandpa! Nana! Gran! Pops!'

They couldn't hear me.

I shouted even louder – 'MR PURRY PAWS!!!' – and this time, Malcolm waved! In a rush of excitement, I thrust my head through the fence, just to get a few centimetres closer.

'Maccy!' I called. 'I'm here, Maccy! It's gonna be all right!'

But it wasn't all right. Because although my head had somehow gone through the fence, the rest of me wouldn't. And when I pulled back, my head wouldn't come out either. I pushed, I pulled, I squeezed, I wriggled – but I was stuck fast.

Some of the people in the Private Picnic Area were looking in my direction. The Hero must be behind me, but I couldn't twist my head round to see, so I strained my neck to look up at the giant screen next to the stage. The live feed kept cutting frantically between scenes of picnic mayhem, as drones collided in their desperation to spot the new Hero.

'I believe,' said the commentator, 'we will be cutting across to the Hero *any second now!*'

The crowd was still, waiting in hushed anticipation. It was like the moment before the band comes on stage or the players enter the pitch – except no one knew which band or which players.

Suddenly, a drone buzzed down and hovered in front of me, its little camera whirring, zooming, focusing. The meadow was silent. The crowd held its breath. A fifty-metre-wide close-up of my bewildered face, poking through the railings, appeared on screen.

'Ladies and gentlemen!' said the commentator. 'Please welcome – our prophesied Legendary Hero!'

16

4:02 p.m. THURSDAY

17 hours and 58 minutes
until Eternal Damnation

I sat opposite the silver-haired host. A large section of fence was still round my neck, propped up by kneeling officials from the Hero Welcoming Committee. They'd decided to remove the whole panel and bring it on stage, rather than waste time cutting me free while the audience was waiting.

'Ladies and gentlemen,' said the host, 'let's hear it for our new Legendary Hero: *Harley Lenton!*'

The crowd went wild, whooping and whistling and cheering. The official Heroes Band played the official Heroes Anthem. There were fireworks and a laser light show and a trapeze display that symbolised Hope against Adversity (according to the subtitles).

The metal railings weighed heavily on my shoulders.

After a few minutes, the silver-haired host settled back into his comfortable interviewer's chair. Someone stuck a microphone in my face.

'Good afternoon, Harley,' the host said.

'Hi,' I said.

The crowd cheered.

'When did you first realise you were a Legendary Hero?'

'I'm not sure I am.'

The crowd cheered.

'Tell us about young Malcolm, the child you've come to rescue.'

'Well, he's my brother . . .'

The rest of my reply was drowned out by oohing and cooing, as the image on the big screen cut to Malcolm being cute. He was chewing on Pops' glasses and staring in big-eyed wonder at a passing bee.

'Now,' continued the interviewer, 'we understand what a hurry you're in, with the risk of Eternal Damnation and so on. But we're just going to take a few questions from the official Harley Fan Club!'

The image on screen cut to an enclosure behind the stage. It was full of crazy people, dressed head-to-toe in Harley merchandise: Harley hats, Harley scarves, Harley T-shirts, Harley trainers, Harley anoraks, Harley flags . . . Except it wasn't authentic Harley gear. It was blatantly a load of stuff recycled from last week's Idolicles Fan Club. They'd put HARLEY labels over IDOLICLES, but the IDO or the CLES always stuck out because of his Heroically long name.

'Harley! Ooooh!' said a woman in Harley face paint.

'Our first question . . .' She fumbled with her prompt card and tried to breathe, but it was all too much for her and she passed out, starstruck. As a medical team swept in and stretchered her off, another Harley Fan stepped forward to replace her.

'Would you use a sword or a spear or a laser against a battalion of killer moths?' he shouted.

'Not sure,' I replied.

The crowd cheered.

'When you achieve Inlightenment, will you fly all the way to the Fire Exit, or just some of the way?' he shouted.

'All the way, I guess?'

The crowd cheered.

'What's your strategy for not running out of time?'

'Well, maybe if I started *now,* instead of answering pointless questions . . .?'

The crowd cheered louder than ever and chanted my name.

'HAR-LEY! HAR-LEY! HAR-LEY! HAR-LEY!'

The silver-haired host leaned back in his comfortable interviewing chair and crossed his legs. 'Harley, we applaud your enthusiasm. But before you go, there is one more question I must ask – on behalf of some people here today.' He put a serious face on, uncrossed his legs, and leaned forward. 'Some people here this afternoon may be surprised to find their new Hero is . . . *different* to what some people

117

might expect from a *traditional* Hero. What would you say to those people?'

I looked at the crowd. Who were these *people* he was talking about? And what did they mean, *different*? Because I was young? Because I was a girl? What?

At first, I was furious – then I thought it was funny – then I was furious again. I should say something. I should stand up and deliver a legendary, Heroic speech about the foolishness of *some people's* prejudice! Then I remembered I couldn't stand up because of the railings round my neck – and, by this point, the crowd had lost interest. They whooped and cheered as I was whisked away, and an epic supergroup of musical legends ran on to kick off the concert.

Backstage, away from the cameras and microphones, the commentator turned off his smile.

'Don't take any notice of the audience,' he said, as a technician sawed through the fence post above my head. 'They'll cheer anyone, as long they don't have to get off their lazy backsides and do anything themselves. The truth is, young lady, you don't stand a chance. Have you even learned the Rites of the Death Master? I didn't think so. Idolicles learned them and mastered them and remastered them. He's a black-belt, gold-medal, top-of-the-class Death Master! And even without all that knowledge, he'd still have his courage and strength and handsomeness to fall back on. What do you have to fall back on, Miss Lenton?

You don't even have a Loyal Sidekick or a Wise Mentor. And don't imagine I'm saying this just because you're a girl. Do you think the Many-Limbed Optimugoon or the Razor-Elbowed Glockenpard cares if you're a girl? As far as they're concerned, you're just a bucket of chicken nuggets on legs.'

Before I could respond, a curtain was pulled aside to reveal a gaggle of Harley Fans grinning up at us. The silver-haired interviewer flashed his showbiz smile back on.

'Our prophesied Legendary Hero will now be reunited with young Malcolm, who she will soon be rescuing from Death!' he announced. Then he shoved me into the Fan Enclosure and disappeared.

'Meet us at the jetty in ten minutes,' said an official, as Harley Fans surrounded me, begging for autographs and snapping selfies. Someone pinned a rosette on me. It was fluffy and pink and heart-shaped and said 'Brave Hero' in glittery bubble writing.

'Is it true that you're going Back to Life on the same day as inheriting the title of Gatekeeper of North-East Biddumshire?' gushed a breathless admirer.

'Actually, it's the Gatekeeper of *Kesmitherly*,' I said, glaring furiously at their stupid grinning faces. 'And if you don't get out of my way, I'll use my sword and my spear and my laser . . .'

They stepped aside, and I went off to find my family.

17

4:39 p.m. THURSDAY

17 hours and 21 minutes
until Eternal Damnation

I hugged Malcolm, then Gran, then Nana, then Pops, then Grandpa – then Malcolm gave Diddy Dino the biggest hug of all. Nana apologised for the wheelie-bag mishap and I said it was no big deal. (Though obviously, it really was.)

Then Gran and Grandpa started introducing me to my extended family – all the great-aunts and great-great-grandparents, and a thousand more ancestors, young and old, who were chatting and eating and playing in the Private Picnic Area. But Pops and Nana quickly pointed out that saying hello to all of them would *literally* take weeks, and we *literally* had ten minutes. There wasn't time to meet the family, not today.

'Next time, then!' said Grandpa with a twinkle in his eye.

As we walked down to the river, I was surprised at how energetic my grandparents had become. They marched, and danced, and twirled, taking turns to bounce Malcolm along on their shoulders. In the excitement of the last few hours, I'd barely had a chance to think about how much I was going to miss them all. I wished it could be yesterday again, the six of us huddled in the caravan . . . But as I watched them bounding along, I realised they'd left their yesterdays behind. This was their home now.

We arrived at a stony beach. In both directions, the River Betwixt looped away into eternity. It was as long as infinity and at least a mile wide, but its waters were murkier than Grimston's Sweet Relish, so there was no guessing how deep it was. The other side of the river was shrouded in mist and shadows. And somewhere in those misty shadows, the Many-Limbed Optimugoon was waiting, waiting, waiting . . . to arm-wrestle me to death!

'Gran,' I said.

'Yes?' said Gran.

A group of officials from the Hero Welcoming Committee was waiting at the water's edge, next to a small rowing boat. One of them, who was probably the boss because he had a clipboard, kept checking his watch impatiently.

'You know how this is your home now,' I said.

'Yes . . .' said Gran.

I looked at my little brother, happily filling Grandpa's pockets with shingle. Then I looked at the flimsy little boat that was supposedly going to take us over to the creepy darkness on the far shore.

'I had an idea,' I said. 'How about me and Malcolm stay here with you?'

Gran was quiet.

'I'll do all the chores,' I said.

Gran took my hands in hers, as the other grandparents gathered round.

'Of course, we'd love to have you,' she said, without smiling. 'It's just . . . tricky.'

'You and Malcolm are *alive*,' said Grandpa. 'If you stayed, you'd keep getting older.'

'Forever,' said Nana.

'Older and older and older,' said Pops. 'Forever and ever and ever and ever. Your bones crack, your muscles waste away, your brain turns to mush, your heart shrivels, your –'

Gran gave Pops a gentle smack on his arm and he stopped.

'So really, there's no choice,' said Gran, squeezing my hands. 'Staying would be worse than going.'

'Unless you fail your quest and become trapped on the Path of Heroes,' Pops pointed out. 'Or you might fall off the path into the abyss – *Beneath*. That's where the Resentful Beasts are: the sabre-toothed tigers, woolly mammoths, dinosaurs, giant sharks, giant scorpions, disease-ridden algae, and all those other creatures desperate for revenge against humanity for hunting them and destroying their habitat and driving them to extinction. They're all waiting down there to rip you and bite you and sting you and poke you, over and over and over – and they never get bored of it! In fact, they love it so much that time is slowed down *Beneath*, to make the eternity of suffering last even longer . . .'

There was an uncomfortable silence. Gran shook her head disapprovingly at Pops.

'We got you a present!' said Grandpa, passing me a big box with a yellow ribbon round it.

'Thanks,' I mumbled. 'Should I open it?'

'Save it for when you get home,' said Nana, with a mysterious twinkle in her eye.

'It's a *gadget*!' said Grandpa, with another great big twinkle in *his* eye. 'We got one of those brainy computer lads to fix it up for you.'

I stood there, still holding the box, which was about the size and weight of Malcolm.

'Do I have to carry it?' I asked. 'All the way along the

Path of . . . you know, the Path?'

'No!' said Pops, whose eyes may also have been twinkling behind his very thick glasses. (These grandparents were so *twinkly* – they loved it down here!)

'And you don't have to carry Maccy either,' said Gran, holding my brother's hands as he bounced his bottom on her feet.

'Because our computer lad also fixed you up a *very modern* transport solution!' said Grandpa. 'And here's the man himself.'

An intense-looking teenager in gold trainers waddled up to us.

'This is J-Wolf,' said Grandpa proudly. 'He built your present *and* your modern transport solution.'

''Sup,' said J-Wolf, holding up his fist in greeting. 'You some next Hero, is it?'

I shrugged.

'Safe.'

Then he shuffled about looking shifty, like a kid who hasn't done his homework.

'So, like, for Idolicles I done a all-terrain moon-buggy with lasers and jet propulsion. But the thing is, his prophecy came early, innit. Not gonna lie, your vehicle was more of a rush job.'

'Is it here? Is it ready? Ooh, I can't wait to see it!' said Grandpa.

J-Wolf looked uncomfortable. I followed his gaze up the beach, towards a pair of technicians in white coats. They were struggling to drag a shopping trolley across the shingle towards us.

'Behold!' said Pops, whose straining eyes hadn't yet focused on what the *modern transport solution* really was.

'Is that . . .?' I asked. 'Are you . . .? Am I . . .?'

Surely they weren't *really* expecting me to push an old trolley along a perilous path of monsters?

'To be fair, Idolicles' one was better,' said J-Wolf. 'But I pimped your ride a bit though, innit.' He pointed to a strand of tinsel wrapped round one end. 'Was gonna give it, like, big woofer speakers, slick wheel trims . . . but you know how it is. Man's busy, innit.'

We all stared at the trolley.

'It's even got a little seat!' said Grandpa. 'You know how Maccy loves to ride the trolley!'

'Look,' I said, anxiously aware that our ten minutes must almost be up, 'could you maybe borrow a phone off somebody, and we could chat about this when I'm on my way?'

'Communicating with the Dead?' Gran chuckled. 'Sounds a bit far-fetched. And you know how muddled Pops gets on the phone, with his squinty eyes and his sausage fingers.'

'Anyway, you can't go yet,' said Nana. 'You've got to

wait for your Guide.'

'My what now?'

'Your Guide,' said Grandpa. 'That nice lad, Oliver. A Visionary's Guide receives the honour of rowing the Legendary Hero across the River Betwixt to the Gateway.'

'You're kidding me.'

'And he did such a good job, guiding you down here.'

'So much quicker than us oldies.'

'That's why we recommended him to the Guide Selection Committee.'

'Not that *he* knew that, of course!'

'Don't worry, Harley. He'll be here soon. Just bide your time.'

'I haven't got *time*!' I snapped, grabbing Malcolm and storming down the beach. 'I'm not *dead*!'

18

4:52 p.m. THURSDAY

17 Hours and 8 minutes
until Eternal Damnation

Somehow, I managed to storm slap-bang into the Hero Welcoming Committee, knocking three of them over and breaking the boss man's clipboard.

'Harrumph!' he said, as his colleagues helped him up. 'Now listen here, Miss Lenton: we need to get some things straight.' He brushed himself down and took charge of the situation. 'Usually, a Legendary Hero would spend a few precious hours studying the Rites of the Death Master *before* attempting the Path of Heroes. Of course, a *True* Hero could simply rely on her courage and cleverness for riddle-solving and beast-battling – and not getting her head stuck in a fence . . .'

Several committee members snickered at this mean comment and a pair of slobbery Doubts phlooomped on to my back.

'Hey!' I said. 'I thought these were banned?'

'Only as far as the river,' said the committee leader, sighing impatiently. 'Haven't you read the brochure? We're past the high-tide mark here, Miss Lenton. Outside the Banned Zone. There'll be plenty of Doubts and Regrets from here onwards, so you'd better get used to being squashed if you're not feeling confident.' He paused to tick some boxes on the crumpled form dangling from his broken clipboard. Judging from his expression, they weren't boxes that said how brilliantly I was doing.

I considered going back up the beach to make the Doubts disappear, like when Olly dragged me into the Banned Zone earlier. But my grandparents were trudging down to join us now, so I decided to just wait and see what craziness would happen next.

'Now as I was saying,' said the committee leader, looking up from his clipboard. 'Because you wasted so much time *showing off* at the picnic, it is too late for you to learn the Rites of the Death Master before you set off. So you'll just have to take them with you.'

A forklift truck moved slowly along the beach and stopped in front of us.

'How you planning to shift this?' asked the driver,

switching off her flashy orange light and nodding towards the huge stone tablet strapped to the forks. The slab was two metres high, a metre wide, and thicker than a proper dictionary. No child could possibly have budged it. Perhaps an Olympic weightlifter might've shunted it along a bit – but even then, it would've sunk the rowing boat.

Etched into the stone's smooth surface were the Rites of the Death Master. At a glance, these Rites looked like detailed instructions on how to complete the Twelve Tasks, plus a few lines of advice about fighting beasts and maintaining a good standard of personal hygiene during a quest. It was written in a very dull style, in tiny writing, with no paragraph breaks. I wasn't sorry there was no time to study it.

'Your first Heroic Deed,' announced an official committee spokesperson, 'shall be to drag the Rites of the Death Master to the Jetty of Destiny, placing it henceforth into the water-bound vessel, known to all who sail within her as ye most glorious Boat of Ages . . .'

I took out my phone and snapped a photo of the stone tablet.

The committee gasped and retreated into a huddle of disappointed muttering, tut-tutting, and head-shaking.

'Kids these days!'

'Lazy.'

'I'll eat my hat if she completes the Twelve Tasks.'

'I'll eat my hat and your shoes if she completes even *one* of the Tasks.'

'I'll eat *your* hat and *my* shoes and *everyone's* lunch if she even makes it *to* the First Task.'

'She'll fall *Beneath* in no time.'

'My soothsayer reckons she's got more chance of growing horns and a tail than making it to the Fire Exit.'

'Ooh, she's *nothing* like Brave Idolicles!'

I felt the Doubts piling on again. And they weren't just on me. The entire Hero Welcoming Committee was covered in them.

'Don't take any notice,' said Gran, putting a comforting hand on my shoulder and leading me away. 'You'll be fine once you achieve Inlightenment.'

The other grandparents nodded their agreement.

'Enlightenment?' I said. 'Is that the flying trick they mentioned in the interview?'

'Yes!' said Gran. 'But it's not *En*lightenment, it's *In*lightenment. *En*lightenment is something else altogether. To achieve Inlightenment, you must place your trust in a truth that fear has hidden deep within you.'

'Okay,' I said. 'What truth?'

'You must search within yourself,' said Nana. 'And there will be much uncertainty. Indeed, trusting this truth will feel dangerous, reckless, foolish, mad!'

'But in your heart,' said Gran, 'you will know it is a

risk worth taking. For once you overcome your fears and doubts, it will make things so much easier for you. An immense weight will be lifted – and you will fly!'

'So Inlightenment will make me lighter? Light enough to fly?'

'Perhaps it would help if I explain the science,' said Grandpa. 'When a Living Visionary achieves Inlightenment, their Body temporarily becomes lighter than their Soul, and the metaphysical differential causes them to *rise up* – like a helicopter, but less twirly-whirly.'

Inlightenment sounded brilliant! But before I could begin searching deep within myself, the fake-imaginary-actually-dead-boy-who-kept-coming-back shouted in my ear.

'Oy! Oy! Oy! Harley-arley-arley *the Legendary Hero*! Who'd have thunk it, eh? Vroom VROOM *VROOOOOM*!!! Me old mucker, a *proper Hero*! Nice one!'

'Your Guide's here,' said Gran.

'Thank you,' I said. 'I noticed.'

'What's that lot up to?' asked Olly, nodding towards the committee. As I looked over, everyone in the huddle raised their hands. Then the group parted, and the boss man marched up to me.

'Harley Lenton. As Acting General Secretary of the Hero Welcoming Committee, it is my duty to inform you that the committee has voted unanimously to withdraw its sponsorship of your quest. Unfortunately, everything we have seen this afternoon suggests that your earlier claim was correct: you are *not* in fact the prophesied Legendary Hero. Clearly an administrative error has occurred.'

'Okay, fine,' I said, hoping this would mean they'd go away. My grandparents and Olly gathered around me protectively.

'I'm not sure you fully understand,' said the Acting General Secretary. He stood his ground, and the rest of the committee formed a defensive semicircle behind him. 'Without official sponsorship, you cannot set foot upon the Path of Heroes. If you attempt to do so, you, and anyone travelling with you, will be deleted in an instant.'

I looked at Malcolm. He was strapped in the trolley seat making choo-choo train noises, apparently eager to get going.

'Deleted?'

'Obliterated. Expunged. Wiped out. You will cease to exist – dead or alive.'

'How dare you!' bellowed Gran, scaring the committee with a finger-wagging that could've silenced a volcano. 'You take that back! Harley *is* a Legendary Hero! She's got more heroism in her big toe –'

'You're bound to say that,' said the Acting General Secretary, peeping out from behind his broken clipboard. 'You're her family. Most grandparents think their grandchildren are special. It's all very sweet and lovely, but it's completely irrelevant. The decision of the committee is final and cannot be overturned without Proof of Heroism. Good day to you.'

He gestured to the committee members to gather their belongings and follow him up the beach.

'That's right, run away!' yelled Pops. 'You chicken-livered, no-good pen-pushers! What did *you* all die of, eh? A nasty paper cut? A scary filing cabinet? Or were you bored to death by the sound of your own voices?'

'Come on, Harley,' said Gran. 'You get on that boat. A Legendary Hero doesn't have to listen to some whiny committee.'

'You sure?' I asked.

'Yes, go on.'

I turned towards the boat.

'FREEZE!'

A security guard leapt in front of me. He was waving a light-sabre-taser-sword kind of electric-stabbing-death-stick-weapon that throbbed with dangerous-looking energy.

'Seriously?' I asked. But I also stopped walking.

'Without sponsorship, you and your brother will be deleted,' repeated the Acting General Secretary from a safe distance at the top of the beach. 'In fact, it might be a good idea to delete you anyway – for giving Heroism a bad name!'

Pops and Grandpa were fuming. Nana and Gran cracked their knuckles and clenched their fists. You could've cut the atmosphere with a laser-death-wand.

But none of us moved. Deletion sounded serious.

19

5:13 p.m. THURSDAY

16 hours and 47 minutes until Eternal Damnation

The tension was electric. Nearly as electric as the magic-wand-radiation-poking-death-rod-thing pointing straight at me. Nobody spoke. Nobody moved.

Then Olly wandered casually in front of it.

There was a gasp from the committee. The electro-stabbing-death-wand crackled menacingly.

'I don't get it,' said Olly, spinning his yo-yo. 'If Harley *ain't* the prophesied Legendary Hero, how come she's got all the Heroic Possessions?'

The Acting General Secretary looked confused and a little worried. Whatever craziness Olly was up to, he'd certainly got the committee's attention.

'Oliver Polliver, at your service,' said Olly, curtseying and bowing. 'I'm a big supporter of the Hero Welcoming Committee. Very grateful for all the hard work you do.'

The Acting General Secretary blushed proudly, then looked confused and worried again. 'What were you saying about the Heroic Possessions?'

'Heroic Possessions? Oh, nothing. I mean you'd know best. You're the experts, after all. It's just I was wondering how come she's got the Possessions of the Legendary Hero if she ain't actually the Legendary Hero.'

'What possessions?'

Olly grabbed my rucksack and rummaged through it, pulling out my hoodie, the rolled-up *Risborough Gazette* and the half packet of chocolate biscuits. He stared at these random items in awe.

'What's it like?' he breathed, turning to me, wide-eyed.

'What's what like?' I said.

'Being a Legendary Hero. What's it *feel* like?'

'Well, I'm not one –'

'Oh, you *are*! Look.' He arranged the contents of my bag ceremoniously upon the beach. Everyone edged forward to see. 'This young lady,' continued Olly, lowering his voice to a near-whisper for dramatic effect, 'is not only the new Gatekeeper of Kesmitherly.'

'Oooooh!' said one committee member, drawn in by

Olly's theatrical delivery.

'She is also a brave warrior!'

'Aaaaah!' said two committee members. Olly really was quite the showman.

'A mage!'

'Ooooh!' said most of the committee members, as the impact of Olly's performance spread like an entertaining virus.

'A healer!'

'Aaaah!' They were all joining in now.

'*And* she is the keeper of . . . the Tunic of Qu'architi-Nu!'

Several people gasped as Olly held my hoodie above his head. For a strange moment, even *I* half believed it had some kind of mystical power.

'Also, she is the keeper of . . . the Biscuits of Paphiphony!'

Olly held the half-empty packet of chocolate biscuits aloft. The spectators were stunned. Again, I found myself wondering if perhaps these biscuits really *were* special? I'd bought them in Meg's Mini Mart, so it didn't seem very likely. But these people seemed convinced . . . I barely noticed a couple of smaller Doubts slipping off my shoulders and plopping into the cloudy water.

'Finally, my old mate Harley, this Legendary Hero what you see before you, is the one and only keeper of . . . the Scroll of REG PROCTOR!'

Olly majestically raised the rolled-up *Risborough Gazette*. He looked like a young King Arthur with the sword of Excalibur, only with a crumpled newspaper and luminous socks. As the committee gawped in wonder, I wasn't sure what to think. I knew it was just an ordinary local newspaper, and I knew Reg Proctor was just an ordinary journalist writing about bin collections – but Olly's performance was so convincing, he'd almost fooled *me*.

'Ladies and jellymen!' Olly went on, making everyone laugh with his amusing use of the wrong word. 'Please put your hands together for my amazing friend, the Legendary Hero: *Harley Lenton!*'

The committee applauded and cheered – some even whooped – and all their Doubts plopped off into the river.

'Wait a minute,' said a suspicious-looking official who had not been cheering. 'I've never heard of any of these things.' The beach was silent. The suspicious committee member thrust his suspicious moustache menacingly into my face. 'This so-called Tunic of Kwaka-Chaka-Noo thing. Where did you get it?'

I gulped. I had a feeling the outlet mall on the edge of Risborough wasn't the right answer.

Olly stifled a giggle, and the suspicious moustache swung round to him.

'What?' snapped the man, whiskers quivering.

'No disrespect, mate,' said Olly, grinning, 'but it *is* a bit of a joke. A member of the official Hero Welcoming Committee who hasn't heard of the Tunic of Qu'architi-Nu! The *legendary* tunic that Harley won in the battle of, you know, against the . . . Mongoose . . . Biker Gang . . . in the Fields of Bleh-minster!'

'The what?'

'Sorry, mate. It's just I thought you was a professional. Bit embarrassing!'

Nana chuckled. Malcolm giggled. Pops guffawed, Gran hooted, Grandpa tittered. And when the rest of the committee saw the Acting General Secretary chortling, they all joined in, laughing at the Moustache Member until he stormed off in a sulk.

Things moved quickly after that. The committee formally reinstated my Hero status, and the security guard with the laser-poker-thing hurried away to deal with another incident. Five minutes later, I was sitting in the boat, facing Olly at the oars. A trolley with a bit of scraggy tinsel tied round one end, containing a big gift with a yellow bow, a rucksack of Heroic Possessions, and a little boy with a cuddly dinosaur, was wedged between us. As we set off towards the opposite shore, the crowd of onlookers cheered us on our way.

'Good luck!' shouted Grandpa.

'Give your mum and dad a kiss from us!' shouted Nana.

'And put your tunic on!' called Gran. 'You'll catch your death!'

From the middle of the river, the well-wishers on the sun-soaked shore of the Happy Meadow had become tiny specks. I wiped away an unheroic tear. If everything went according to plan, this was the last I'd see of my grandparents for a lifetime. I knew how lucky I'd been, getting to see them again – but it hadn't been long enough. I never even got to talk to them about their stories being real, about lying to Mum and Dad, about whether the

Gatekeeper to a Portal of Doom had to work weekends, about where to buy *Special Teabags*, about how to do my maths homework . . .

I guess it could never be long enough.

Opposite me, on the other side of a trolley, Olly was rowing and talking and talking and talking. Behind him, our destination was shrouded in an eerie darkness that made me shudder every time I looked at it, as if icy fingers were reaching across the murky river and grasping my heart. When I closed my eyes, the steady splish-splashing of the oars was almost soothing – if only Olly could've stopped talking for *one second.*

'Of course, you knew, and I knew, and your grandparents knew, that them Heroic Possessions was only normal things – even that committee knew, really. But none of them dared admit it in case they was wrong. What I done, see, I used their pride against them . . .'

'Yeah, it was clever. Thanks for saving us,' I mumbled. And I meant it – I was just a bit distracted, thinking about what awaited us *over there . . .*

'Now I'm assuming you want me as your sidekick?' Olly went on. 'Only, you ain't officially requested my assistance. But just so you know, I *am* up for it. I mean, here I am, rowing you over to the Path of Heroes so you can save your strength for all the clever-clogs stuff. This is exactly the sort of thing a Loyal Sidekick does –'

And suddenly, for a mad moment, I wondered if maybe it *would* be helpful to have Olly along . . .

'– and it'll be wicked 'cos I'll do karate on the dragons. *And* I've got Special Skills. No word of a lie! I'm *gifted.* Oy! Oy!'

Then I remembered: Olly meant Trouble. I thought back to all those afternoons outside Miss Stemper's office – the look on Mum's face after I melted her shoes – the tragic fate of those poor garden gnomes . . . Having Olly as a sidekick was an insane idea.

'. . . I'm gonna tell you something now that is *top secret.* This must not leave this boat. I, Oliver Polliver, can Summon the Beasts! I mean, I can't *completely* do it, but almost. And I could be a Brave Martyr – you know, do some kind of sacrifice for the Legendary Hero's Noble Quest! Imagine that! Not bad, eh?'

The gentle rocking motion of the boat had lulled Malcolm to sleep and I wished it would do the same for me. But Olly kept chatting and cracking jokes and singing, and as he rowed us through the miserable fog and into the creepy darkness, the panic was rising inside me. I just needed a moment of calm to think about all the scary stuff that lay ahead – and this boy *would not shut up*!

As we approached the shore, an enormous gateway loomed out of the mist. Olly tethered the boat to a withered tree stump, and together we lifted the trolley on to the bank. It was colder on this side of the river. I put my hoodie on and zipped up Malcolm's onesie. He woke up and said, 'Arwee?'

'I'm here, Maccy,' I said. 'It's okay. Everything's okay.'

But it wasn't okay. The panic was bubbling to the surface. And Olly was still talking – about bears, or javelins, or a magic tree or something. And I was still trying to think – about completing the Twelve Tasks, achieving Inlightenment, not falling *Beneath*, getting Back to Life . . . And he was *still talking* – about an enchanted plum, the joy of Frisbee, and *every other single thing* –

'Just *stop!*' I yelled. 'Stop talking! The answer's *no*. You *can't* come with me, I don't want you to be my sidekick, I don't want a sidekick!'

I had to storm off quite slowly because of the trolley's wonky wheel, but it shut him up.

When I reached the Gateway to the Path of Heroes, I thought about looking back. Would Olly still be there? Would he have waited? Would I say sorry?

I *would* say sorry! I'd overreacted, lost my temper. It was the pressure of being a Legendary Hero – it wasn't Olly's fault. Well, it was a *bit* his fault. But he'd helped me, and he'd help me again. He was my friend. I could turn back now. Apologise. We could work together . . .

I looked back.

But it was too late.

Olly was already halfway across the river. Without me and my trolley weighing it down, the boat skimmed over the water towards the eternal sunshine of a hassle-free death.

PART FOUR

BEYOND THE BACK OF BEYOND

20

6:40 p.m. THURSDAY

15 hours and 20 minutes
until Eternal Damnation

The Path of Heroes was a narrow, rocky ledge clinging perilously to the side of a cliff. To our left, the sheer mountainside stretched up, up, up into ominous darkness. To our right, a pitiless chasm plunged down, down, down into scary clouds below. These clouds hid the inhabitants of *Beneath* from view, but the snarls and screeches echoing from its depths convinced me that falling in would be a bad idea. To make matters worse, the trolley was possessed by demons, hell-bent on dragging us towards the abyss. After a bit, I realised it wasn't demons, it was just the wonky wheel. Somehow, that was even more depressing. At least battling demons would've felt worth the effort.

As I struggled over the rocky ground, I wondered what sort of Task I'd get to fail first. Racing the Swift-Footed Gazellopuss? Bathing the Warty Krustaming? Feeding the Five Thousand Mouths of Gobbo Mawjaw? And after the Spikanik had spiked me, or the Sporgal had skewered me, or the Spifflemucus had suffocated me, would they even bother to swallow me? Or would they just fling me *Beneath*, to the billions of Resentful Beasts waiting to bite and scratch and sting and crush me, again, and again, and again?

Occasionally, part of me wanted to peer over the edge and look deep into those horrible swirling vapours – to stare down those Resentful Beasts and face my fears! But most of me really *didn't* want to do that. So I kept my eyes on the path ahead, and kept walking.

Spooky shadows danced across the rocks as we rolled slowly, wonkily onwards. I got my phone out and looked at the photo of the Stone Tablet, zooming in on the top-left corner.

'The Rites of the Death Master,' it began. 'Be it that thus ye shall know . . .'

My eyes began to close. I shook myself awake and tried again.

'Be it that thus ye shall know . . .'

Again, my eyes were flickering shut. I shook myself, smacked my cheeks, stamped up and down, and tried one more time.

'Be it that thus ye shall know . . .'

I put my phone away. The Rites of the Death Master were just too boring. I'd have to learn them later.

I trekked on. It was hard going, but at least I wasn't weighed down by Doubts and Regrets – they'd all slipped away when Olly had done his Heroic Possessions con-trick at the jetty. He'd really helped me there. If Olly hadn't stepped in, who knows what would've happened?

And it was genuinely impressive how he'd fooled all those committee people. I really should've thanked him more enthusiastically. I certainly shouldn't have shouted at him. I wished I could go back.

PHLOOOMP! SPLURPSH! CRUMPH!

A pack of Regrets seized their moment and leapt on.

I dragged myself onwards, but the weight of the Regrets was slowing . . . me . . . down. Now I'd *never* make it to the Fire Exit on time!

FLOOMPSH! PFURPF! KWOOMPH!

The Doubts pounced. It was too gloomy to see their bright sides.

I lay down in the darkness. Regrets and Doubts piled on.

Worst start to an epic quest ever.

Then I thought of the time when Grefflet the Forgetful went out to slay the Serpent of a Thousand Nightmares without her Sword of Righteousness. And the time when Big Musclius the Confident spilled egg on his chainmail before he'd even lowered the drawbridge . . .

This wasn't the *Worst Start to an Epic Quest Ever.* It was just averagely rubbish.

I grabbed the trolley to pull myself up, and trudged slowly on.

A few minutes later, I was about to stop for a biscuit break, when I noticed a sign on the path ahead. I shuffled towards it.

WELCOME TO THE FIRST OF
THE LEGENDARY TWELVE TASKS.
GOOD LUCK! ☺

I looked around, suspiciously, trying to work out where the monsters were going to ambush me from. Then something scuttled out of the shadows, and I ducked behind the trolley.

After a few minutes of waiting to be eaten, I opened my eyes and stared bravely at the monster. It was small and fluffy with a big head, a tiny body, and just enough legs to make it quirky.

'Woof woof!' said Malcolm, reaching out to try and stroke it.

I crawled out from my hiding place. The creature looked up at me with its big eyes. It was kind of cute. I might've been tempted to give it a pat on the head if I wasn't in Battle Mode. But the shame of diving for cover behind my brother made me determined to slay whatever Hell Beast

was guarding the First Task as soon as it appeared.

'Shoo!' I said, suspecting this fluffy thing had been sent as a decoy to distract me. The creature shook its big head, and I noticed it was wearing a collar. Keeping my wits about me, I bent down and looked at the tag.

'Beast Guardian of the First Task,' I read. '*You?*'

The Beast Guardian of the First Task looked up at me with its big eyes. This was the first real monster I'd ever seen, and it was a big disappointment. Well, a small disappointment. And a big relief, to be honest. It had no claws, no horns, no teeth. It didn't even have a mouth. If all the monsters were as small and harmless as this one, I'd have nothing to fear!

'What do I do, Beast Guardian of the First Task?' I asked.

It pointed towards the sign with a soft paw. Below the welcome message, green letters appeared on an olden-days computer screen: TASK INCOMPLETE.

'So what do I do?' I asked again. The Beast shrugged. It still didn't have a mouth.

Behind the sign, a light bulb sat on a small table. A stepladder stood beside it, and an unlit bulb dangled on a cable from the darkness above.

It seemed obvious what I needed to do. But was the First Task of the Legendary Hero *really* changing a light bulb? I looked at the evidence again: burnt-out old bulb, fresh new bulb, stepladder. What else could it be?

I hugged Malcolm and did my secret celebration dance (the Victory Shuffle). This was the best news I'd had in months. I was an expert light-bulb-changer! I was a black-belt, gold-medal, top-of-the-class light-bulb-changer! I'd changed *loads* of light bulbs! All this time, I'd been worrying about *classic* epic challenges – wrestle a bear, outrun a stag, slay a dragon – and all I had to do was change a light bulb! Twelve Tasks in fifteen hours? No problem!

I felt twenty kilos lighter as the Regrets popped and the Doubts shrivelled. Suddenly everything made sense. The months of friendlessness – the boredom, the loneliness – *it all made sense.* If I'd been having fun with friends for the last year and a half, I'd never have spent so many hours and hours helping my parents with household chores. I'd never have learned how to wire a plug, fix a puncture, bleed a radiator, change a toilet roll, empty a bin . . .

Finally, my destiny had revealed itself. The Tasks were going to be epically boring! The kind of epically boring chores that some twelve-year-olds might've struggled with. But not Harley the Legendary Hero. With my general maintenance skills, I really *could* rescue my little brother from Eternal Damnation!

I opened the stepladder, climbed up it, removed the burnt-out bulb, climbed down, placed the old bulb on the table, put the new bulb in my pocket, and climbed back up.

One step, two steps, three steps, four steps . . .

. . . five steps, six steps, seven steps . . .

Something wasn't right. The first time I'd gone up, the stepladder had had five steps. I stopped. The light-fitting was just above me, swaying gently out of reach. One step away. The ladder had one step left. I stepped up and reached again. The light-fitting was still out of reach – still one step away. I stepped again. Still couldn't reach.

Glancing at the path below, my head spun, and I gripped the ladder tightly.

The ground was twenty metres away. The ladder had grown.

Its feet were only a short distance from the edge of the chasm. If I fell from here, I wouldn't just break a leg, or an arm, or a head. I'd fall *BENEATH*. To be ripped and slashed and torn forever and ever into tiny pieces by a billion ravenous beasts. To be nipped, and stung, and poked, and clawed – over and over and over.

Slowly, carefully, I climbed down the ladder. As I descended, the ladder shrank, and the light-fitting followed me down, so I could still nearly . . . almost . . . reach it . . .

I looked away, pretending to notice something in the distance. Then, suddenly, I lunged upwards, to take the light-fitting by surprise. It rose calmly out of reach –

teasing me.

The ladder wobbled, and I climbed back down.

Again, the ladder shortened with me, and the light-fitting followed me down, always *just out of reach.*

I stepped off the bottom rung on to firm ground. I looked up at the light-fitting, hanging there, waiting for me to go again. I looked at the display.

TASK INCOMPLETE.

I looked at Malcolm, swinging his legs and chatting to Diddy Dino.

I looked at my phone. The battery was dying, and time was racing on. I should've finished this Task by now. I should be on my way to the Descaling a Kettle Task, or the Replacing a Vacuum-Cleaner Bag Task, or whatever mundane chore I needed to do next to get out of this place.

I thought about asking the Beast for a clue, maybe bribing it with a biscuit.

'Why don't you get a mouth?' I yelled.

Malcolm did a sad face. He didn't like me shouting at the fluffy thing.

The Beast Guardian pointed at the sign. The screen flickered and TASK INCOMPLETE was replaced by CLUE: PLEASE WAIT.

I waited, gripping the light bulb with a desperate hope.

CHANGE BULB.

I frowned, waiting for the display to change again.

It didn't.

'*Aaaaaaaagghhh!!!*'

In a fit of rage, I hurled the bulb at the jagged mountainside, where it smashed into smithereens.

'Oh no, no, no, no! What have I done!?' I gasped, frantically trying to piece together the tiny fragments.

It was several minutes before I noticed the screen, which now flashed between the messages BULB CHANGED and TASK COMPLETE.

And it was several more minutes before I'd calmed down enough to realise I had, indeed, changed the bulb. Completely.

One down, eleven to go.

The display changed again.

TIME: 23 MINUTES.

BEST HERO TIME: 8 SECONDS.

23 MINS NOT BAD, CONSIDERING.

Now the *sign* was mocking me!

'Considering *what*?' I scowled back. But before I could get into an argument with a sarcastic 1980s computer, the Beast Guardian of the First Task gave me a smiley *Well Done* sticker. Then it pointed to the bottom of the sign and scuttled away.

I hadn't noticed the small print before. At the bottom of the sign in a teeny-tiny font were the words: *To avoid unnecessary delay, please refer to the Rites of the Death Master for guidance on all Tasks.*

I sighed, gave Malcolm the sticker, and got my phone out.

Looked like I'd have to do my Heroic Homework after all.

21

7:28 p.m. THURSDAY

14 hours and 32 minutes
until Eternal Damnation

'Be it that thus ye shall know . . . *LOW BATTERY.*'

Whoa! The idea of a dead phone in the underworld was too horrible to imagine. I took a deep breath and launched myself into a burst of superfast speedreading.

'Be it that thus ye shall know, the righteous may verily smite the unworthy . . . *DAD CALLING.*'

The battery died and my phone switched itself off.

'*NOOOOO!!!!*' I yelled, verily smiting my unworthy trolley with righteous anger. 'Why now, Dad? Why call me now? And why didn't I read the stupid Rites of the stupid

Death Master before? And what's the point of smashing a light bulb anyway?'

I could've gone on, but a pack of grim-looking Regrets had gathered in front of me.

'Come on, then!' I said, through gritted teeth, tensing against the impact of their slobberiness. But they didn't move. They just sat there, pulsating and looking dribbly.

Suddenly, I charged at them with the trolley, squashing one and kicking another against a rock. A big Regret flung itself at me, but I was too quick. My fist burst through its blubbery belly so that I was wearing it like a huge, sloppy bracelet. I let its squidgy carcass slide off my wrist.

'No. More. Regrets.'

The rest of the flock made a swift, squelchy retreat.

'Hey there! Welcome to the Second Task!' said a floppy-fringed giant stick insect in a shiny suit, handing me a glossy leaflet. 'My name's Colin, and I'll be your adviser for this Task. Have you ever oiled a squeaky door before?'

'What's the trick, Colin?' I grabbed him by the collar, pulling his stupid grinning face down to my level. 'I'm not messing about, Colin. Tell me the trick.'

'There's no trick!'

'Don't push me, Colin.'

'Honest, there's no trick! Please don't hurt me! It's not l-l-like that l-l-light bulb one. That's pesky, I know, but –'

'*Colin!*'

'Look, I'll d-d-do it for you.'

Colin produced an oil can from his floppy sleeve and oiled the door.

'Congratulations! You have completed the Second Task in a record-breaking thirty-four seconds. It only remains for me to wish you a pleasant journey . . .'

I marched proudly along the Path of Heroes, feeling invincible. I'd beaten the Regrets and Doubts into submission. I'd bullied a monster into doing the Second Task for me.

And now I was about to achieve Inlightenment.

All I had to do was place my trust in a truth that fear had hidden deep within me. A truth that would feel mad and dangerous but would make things easier. And that unexpected truth had just revealed itself.

Violence *was* the answer, after all!

I did a hop, skip and jump, half expecting to take off. I wasn't quite flying yet, but I felt floaty. I was eighty per cent certain that this violence idea must be my hidden truth. Soon enough, my Body would be lighter than my Soul, and I'd fly! All I needed to do was fight and threaten my way along the Path of Heroes to the Fire Exit. These pathetic little fluffballs and skinny insects would be no match for Harley the Legendary Hero!

And if it worked down here, then why not up there

too? Plenty of people believed in fighting and aggression. Kids, adults, animals, governments . . . *millions* believed in violence! Violence could get you what you wanted, violence could defeat evil, violence could make you a True Hero!

I arrived at a tombstone with the words *Third Task* engraved on it in Gothic script.

'Reveal yourself, Beast!' I shouted.

A hairy claw the size of a beagle emerged from the freshly dug grave. It was attached to a scarred and blistered arm like a muscular tree trunk. Another gore-drenched arm followed, and the Beast Guardian of the Third Task dragged itself from the pit and loomed over me. Its clammy breath smelt like rancid meat. Flies buzzed in and out of its cavernous nostrils. The horns on its head had horns, and even the horns' horns had horns. The slobbering Beast was so huge and repulsive, it took several minutes for me to find my voice again.

'Hi,' I mumbled, deciding to shelve the *violence is the answer* plan for the time being. I could always come back to it later, if I was confronted by something smaller and weaker.

The Beast Guardian of the Third Task beckoned me with a crooked claw. As it stomped over to a door in the cliffside, the ground vibrated beneath us. It was a thick, heavy, iron door, a damp-dungeon-in-a-creepy-castle door. As the Beast heaved it open, the hinges screeched like a bat stubbing its toe. I thought about recommending Colin and his oil can, but decided to save the small talk.

The door opened on to a long, broad corridor. Flaming torches hung on each stone wall, dramatically lighting a gallery of posh old paintings and tapestries.

'Straighten them!' bellowed the Beast.

'Huh?' I said. The Beast nodded towards the walls, then sat down with an earth-shattering thump and began sharpening its claws with an axe.

I pushed the trolley down the hallway, examining the pictures. There was an occasional misty landscape with a dragon dying in the distance, but mostly they were full-length portraits of serious-looking Legendary

Heroes. A lot of the names on the inscriptions were familiar from my grandparents' stories. Here was Bilbamýn the Bold, hacking at the Many-Limbed Optimugoon with his massive sword. Here was Hallyria the Unrelenting, feeding the Five Thousand Mouths of Gobbo-Mawjaw. Here was Vileeda the Valiant, soothing the Razor-Elbowed Glockenpard with her enchanted flute before she wrestled it to death. And here, once again, was Craemog the Intrepid, fearlessly slaying the slippery Mega-Worm – although this Craemog was a lot older and chubbier than the actor in the movie version.

It was a tremendous Heroes Gallery. In Paris or New York, people would've paid good money to stand in front of these old pictures.

But they were all wonky.

Bilbamýn the Bold was teetering to the right. Vileeda the Valiant was leaning to the left.

Craemog the Intrepid was nearly okay, but not quite, so that I had to step back and squint to work out whether he needed to go up a bit this side or that side. I went up and down the corridor, trying to straighten them all – but as soon as Bilbamýn stopped looking wonky, Vileeda seemed to be tilting again. The dancing shadows from the flickering torches didn't help, but the lighting wasn't the main problem.

'You need help,' growled the Beast Guardian, in a voice like distant thunder.

'Yes, please,' I said, hoping for a better clue than last time.

The Beast shook like a small earthquake and snorted a flurry of moths out of its nostrils. This went on for a while before I realised it was laughing.

'You need a sidekick,' it tremored. 'One of you adjusts the picture, while the other stands back and says, "Up a bit, down a bit, up a bit." That's how you straighten pictures.'

I wanted to flick the monster's stupid face. *Obviously* that was how you straightened pictures. Of all people, *I* knew how to straighten pictures. Doing boring household chores was my superpower; that's the kind of Legendary Hero I was. But I didn't have a sidekick to help me. I only had Malcolm, and he'd be no good at this even if he was awake.

In the end, I decided against flicking the monster and just got on with straightening the pictures the slow way. Down a bit, step back, look at it, go up to it again and put it up a bit, step back, look at it, go up to it and put it down a bit. For more than an hour, I went up and down the hallway, adjusting the dusty old canvases until, eventually, they were all hanging straight. With a helper, I could've done the whole corridor in a few minutes.

'Task complete!' quaked the Beast. Then it lumbered down the corridor, putting every picture back on the wonk.

'Imagine having that job!' I muttered as I wheeled the trolley back to the Path of Heroes.

Behind me, the Beast roared. This was a classic *run away now* situation, but curiosity overcame fear. I couldn't resist turning to see what would swarm out of its angry nostrils this time. But nothing did. The Beast sighed like an avalanche, and a shimmering teardrop – like an immense diamond in the flickering torchlight – crept down its scarred, leathery cheek.

I hadn't enraged the Beast; I'd made it cry.

'You're right!' the Beast thundered between sobs. 'My job *is* terrible! So pointless! Such a waste of everyone's time! I put them wonky, Heroes try and straighten them, I put them wonky again. This isn't what I dreamed of, you know, as a young Beast in my mother's tentacles . . .'

I slipped away, feeling even less Heroic than usual.

22

8:57 p.m. THURSDAY

13 hours and 3 minutes
until Eternal Damnation

Three down, nine to go. But if all the Tasks took as long as the wonky pictures one, I'd never make it out in time. I'd be trapped here for eternity, my brain would turn to mush, my heart would shrivel . . .

I needed to speed up. No point wondering if I'd be better off with a sidekick; I didn't have one and that was that. Anyway, unlike picture-straightening, most things were easier *without* other people. Other people always wanted to chat, and join in, and get involved.

But I was getting tired, and the trolley was getting heavier, and my wrists were aching from constantly steering to the left. It felt unfair. None of the old Heroes had to push a trolley. They just handed their luggage to a sidekick and sat back to enjoy the journey on a magic carpet or a golden chariot or a giant eagle.

A couple of blubbery Regrets and a fat Doubt were hanging about, but they didn't approach. News of my road-rage must have spread. However, despite this small triumph for kicking and punching, I'd gone right off the *violence is the answer* idea. It just wasn't my style. I realised that even if I could've slain that last Beast Guardian, I wouldn't have. I felt bad enough about making it cry. And I felt thoroughly ashamed about how I'd treated poor Colin. Heroism was no excuse for bullying.

My search for Inlightenment would continue. If violence wasn't the answer, I'd have to look elsewhere for the hidden truth that would make me fly.

I knew my parents would've approved. They hated any kind of violence. Dad had to leave the room when Gran and Nana watched the wrestling on Christmas Day, and Mum nearly cried when Olly filmed me dropping all the different fruits out of my bedroom window. Watermelon was best. Smashed to pieces like an exploding head.

Mmmm, watermelon.

Mum and Dad would've eaten their takeaway by now. Munched and chewed and slurped and gobbled their noodles or chips or rice or chicken all greasy and salty and hot and sweet . . .

I stopped food-dreaming before I ate my own tongue, and grabbed the chocolate biscuits from my rucksack. I'd been saving them, just in case they really did have magical powers. I mean, I knew Olly had made all that *Biscuits of Paphiphony* stuff up, but I guess I'd become more superstitious since the discovery of a Portal of Doom in my grandparents' toilet.

Weirdly though, now that I had the chocolate biscuits in my hand, I felt too hungry to eat them. In fact, I was *so* hungry, that when a floating pizza turned up, I followed it. I put the biscuits in my pocket and followed the floating pizza, even though I had a strong suspicion it was an *evil* floating pizza, sent to tempt me away from my quest.

The pizza lured me off the Path of Heroes, through spooky trees, between creepy bushes, and past a sign that read, *Don't Go Down Here!* I knew I shouldn't, but still I followed. Who wouldn't? It was a floating pizza!

When the route back to the Path of Heroes had disappeared, the pizza stopped, tore a slice of itself off, and presented itself to me. I ate it, and it was the most delicious pizza I'd ever eaten – with only the slightest aftertaste of evil.

Then it began to snow. Fat, soft, fluffy snowflakes, settling instantly upon the warm ground. I made a snow heap, a snow mound and a snow pile. The snow was warm. Lovely, warm snow.

As I helped myself to chocolates from the chocolate trees, sweets from the sweet trees and mangoes from the mango vending machine, I had a feeling something wasn't quite right. But a playlist of my favourite tunes was massaging my ears, so I brushed my worries aside and relaxed in the warm snow. This is what life's all about! I thought, lying back to enjoy the firework display, the smell of the barbecue and the breeze that seemed to be singing, 'Harley's great! Woo-hoo, Harley's the best!'

When I stood up to leave, a comfy beanbag shuffled under me, and I flopped into its soft embrace. A gentle breeze danced beneath the warm sun, and a palm tree drifted over to shade me when it became half a degree too hot. Kindly snow-aunties played with Malcolm in a den made of cupcakes. They changed his nappy, gave him a drink, made Diddy Dino talk in a funny voice.

Everything was floating – just a little bit – drifting and bobbing *just enough* to provide the perfect buoyancy for total relaxation. I took the dead phone out of my rucksack and connected it to a charger, hovering beside me.

I closed my eyes.

No point rushing through Eternity.

Clearly, this enchanted place was trying to delay me. I realised this, but I felt blissfully powerless to resist its temptations. It was just like Bilbamýn the Bold's encounter with the mermaids, or Craemog the Intrepid's forty nights in the cheese shop.

But I had learned from their mistakes. I knew I'd be fine, as long as I was careful *not to fall asleep.*

HARLEY'S DREAM

A play in one act, devised and performed by the Spirits of the Living. With additional dialogue by Harley's Brain.

Enter Mum and Dad, on a cloud, from above.

MUM:

You must achieve Inlightenment, oh Legendary Hero!

DAD:

What will it be? Cuckoo! Tra-lee! What will it be?

MUM:

The wisdom of the Ancients shall set you free!

From a trapdoor, below, enter Miss Stemper.

MISS STEMPER:

Listen to me!

Enter Bess, flapping a large blue sheet to represent water.

BESS:

Wanna go Splash Madness?

MISS STEMPER:

Never wear socks with sandals!

MUM:

Sharing is caring!

MISS STEMPER:

Running with scissors makes Jack a
dull boy!

DAD:

Slow and steady loses the race!

MUM:

Just go for it, Harley! If you believe,
you can do anything!

Enter a Giant Caterpillar. Mum feeds it a
strawberry, a pickle, some cheese and a
sausage, but it's still hungry. Harley starts
eating the food as well, then realises that
SHE is now the caterpillar.

Enter Harley's grandparents. They are each
holding a cartoon bomb with a sizzling fuse.
Harley tries to warn them, but her mouth is too
full of strawberry, pickle, cheese and sausage.

The grandparents explode in four puffs of
smoke and are replaced by four more giant
caterpillars. They creep slowly, menacingly
towards her. Harley tries to run, but she's
buried up to her neck in warm snow . . .

I woke with a jerk. I wasn't buried in snow and I wasn't stuffed with pickle – but the giant caterpillar monsters really *were* creeping towards me! I jumped up and waved my worn-out *Risborough Gazette* threateningly. The caterpillars slithered on through the warm snow – which gave me an idea.

'Oy!' shouted the nearest giant caterpillar, as the first of my precision-targeted snow grenades exploded on impact. It was a surprising reaction for a Deadly Beast, but I didn't let it put me off. I reloaded and struck again, and again, and again.

'Geroff!' yelled the biggest caterpillar.

'Enough already!' squealed the smallest caterpillar.

'Stop it, Harley!' said the fourth caterpillar.

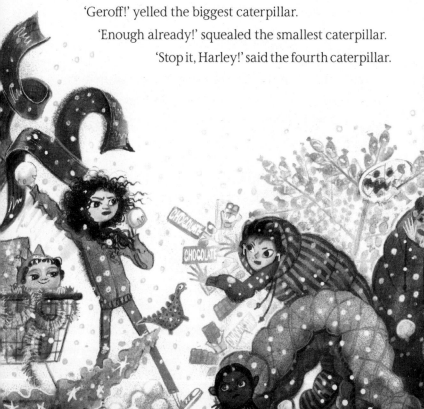

Before I could gather enough ammunition for a fresh bombardment, the hideous creatures metamorphosed in front of me, shedding their skins to reveal humanoid heads!

'Quit luzzing snowballs at us, won't yer!' said the Olly-caterpillar hybrid, shaking snow out of his ears.

'Your friend's a sharp-shooter!' said Frazzle-half-caterpillar.

'She throws like a Hero!' said Elektra-half-caterpillar.

'Epic snowballer!' said Sparky-half-caterpillar.

On closer inspection, I saw that the caterpillar bodies were, in fact, sleeping bags.

'What are you doing here?' I asked. 'And why are you crawling around in sleeping bags?'

'Bag Exception,' declared Olly proudly.

'Dead kids aren't allowed along the Path of Heroes, same as how Living people can't get through the Portal of Doom,' Sparky explained.

'Unless you're *either* a Visionary Hero *or* you use the Bag Exception,' Elektra added.

'We wriggled along in bags, see,' Frazzle clarified. 'Like how your little brother slid down the gloopy chute in your Nana's wheelie bag.'

'We're like hand luggage,' said Sparky. 'But bigger, and with actual hands.'

Olly wriggled up into a sitting position.

'When you had your hissy fit and

sent me packing, I thought, how can I get along there to help her? And that's when I hit upon my genius cunning plan: Why not try the old Bag Exception?'

Olly grinned, pleased with himself.

'Actually, it was my idea,' said Frazzle.

'Yeah, it was Frazzle's idea,' said Sparky and Elektra.

'Whatever,' said Olly. 'Look, Harley-arley-arley, here's the deal. Turns out I'm actually *destined* to be your sidekick. Now I know you might think I'm just some loser dead kid, but I can help you, I really can.'

You had to admire his perseverance. And truthfully, he would've been a real help back there with the pictures. And he *had* guided me through the Nothing and dragged me into the Banned Zone and slithered all the way here in a sleeping bag. And there *had* been a lot of Good Times before the Bad Times (and maybe some of the Bad Times weren't even that Bad) . . .

'Come on, Harley-arley-arley! Just give me one more chance to hang out with a true legend!'

. . . and he was always saying nice things, boosting my confidence, lifting me up . . .

'A true legend who's also *my best friend.*'

But now he'd taken it too far, and I realised this was becoming the cheesiest, slushiest, awkwardest, most embarrassingly soppy nonsense I'd ever heard (and from the looks on their faces, his pylon friends agreed). If Olly carried on like this, I'd *have* to let him be my sidekick – just to make him stop.

'What use are you going to be in a sleeping bag?' I asked.

'Well, here's the thing. If you make me your Official Sidekick to the Legendary Hero, I'm allowed here *not in a bag*. That's the rules, see.'

I looked at my dead friend, sitting there with his grinning face poking out of a sleeping bag.

A pair of scissors floated safely into my hand.

'How d'you do that?' gawped Frazzle. 'You a wizard?'

'You've got to be careful here,' I warned. 'You can get whatever you want.'

'Like wishes?' said Elektra.

'No, it's better than wishes. You don't even need to think about what you want, you just want it and it's there. Seriously, you need to be careful. Getting whatever you want makes it very hard to leave. You'll get stuck here.'

'Is that what happened to you?' asked Sparky.

'No,' I said. 'It won't happen to me. I'm leaving soon.'

'But you've already – *hey*!'

I stuck the scissors through the bottom of Frazzle's sleeping bag and cut a leg-hole. Then I cut another leg-hole and two arm-holes. He poked his limbs through the holes so that he was wearing the bag like a very loose padded leotard. I did the same for the others until the four of them looked like a troupe of arctic gymnasts in hand-me-downs.

'Nice one, Harley!' said Sparky.

'I don't get it, though,' I said. 'You can't have slithered all the way here from the gateway. It's slower than crawling. It would've taken *hours*.'

'It did take hours,' said Sparky.

'Like, eight hours,' said Elektra.

'But I've only been on the path for . . . Oh no! Oh no, no, no!' My heart pounded as I grabbed my floating phone, to see if the worst possible thing that could happen had happened.

It had, of course, happened.

I'd had a good night's sleep.

23

7:00 a.m. FRIDAY

3 hours until Eternal Damnation

I'd slept for more than nine hours on my comfy beanbag – which meant only three hours to complete nine Tasks and pass through the Fire Exit – which meant we were almost certainly destined for Eternal Damnation. There was no way I could get through the remaining Tasks and all the way to the Fire Exit at the rate I'd been going 'til now. To stand any chance of saving Malcolm, I'd have to do things differently.

My first plan, now that my phone was charged, was to finally learn the Rites of the Death Master.

'Be it that thus ye shall know . . .'

But that was just *too boring*, so I put my phone away

and went with plan B instead.

'Olly,' I said. 'Do you know the way back to the Path of Heroes?'

'Course I do.'

'Are you any good at changing plugs and oiling doors and stuff?'

'Course I am.'

'Can you promise to be quiet?'

Olly mimed zipping his mouth shut and nodded. I looked around, weighing up my options. I didn't seem to have any.

'Okay, you can be my sidekick,' I mumbled.

'Oy! Oy! Oy!' shouted Olly, shedding his sleeping bag and emerging like a noisy butterfly. 'You won't regret this, Harley-arley-arley! Vroom *vroom VROOOOOM*!!! My old mucker, my best buddy!'

'Yeah, yeah, whatever. Just get us out of here.'

'I'll be *epically* loyal! I'll be your faithful servant! I'll stay by your side every step of the way, I won't let you down – Blimey, lads. Look up there!'

A huge electricity pylon had appeared in front of us. Nestled among buzzing cables near the top of the tower was a bright red Frisbee.

'Last one up's a pillock!' yelled Olly, running excitedly towards the pylon.

I could almost taste the raw electricity crackling

through the cables. I stepped back. But the high-voltage hum drew the others towards it, like bees to pollen. Olly's friends sprinted after him, the four of them hollering and whooping as they climbed towards the Frisbee.

'Whoa!' gasped Sparky. 'This pylon's awesome!'

'It's a beauty!' said Elektra.

'Woo-hoo!' squealed Frazzle.

'It's not real!' I shouted.

'Wanna come up?' said Olly.

'No!' I said. 'We need to *go . . .*'

'Just give me five minutes!' Olly called back. 'Must get the Frisbee!'

They leapt from strut to strut, dodging between cables throbbing with *DANGER! DANGER! HIGH VOLTAGE!*

'Olly! There's only three hours until my heart starts shrivelling!' I called, but he was too high up to hear.

Suddenly, a shrill whistle cut through the air.

'Police!' yelled Sparky.

'Run!' yelled Frazzle.

An olden-days policeman jogged towards the pylon, blowing his whistle and shouting, 'Oi! Come here, you lot!' The Frisbee kids jumped to the ground and sprinted away as the officer chased them. Olly was ahead of the group, and he soon ducked out of sight. The police officer shook his fist and followed Elektra, Sparky and Frazzle down an alleyway.

'Phoop! Phoop!' said Malcolm, mimicking the policeman's whistle. He crawled towards the big kids' climbing frame, but it disappeared before he got a chance to electrocute himself. He looked disappointed for a moment, then cheered himself up by rolling around in the snow.

I sighed. So much for the sidekick plan. I mean, I wasn't surprised that Olly abandoned me; he'd done it *Before*. And anyway, it was typical giant-caterpillar behaviour – epically loyal until an electricity pylon with a Frisbee on it appears, then off it wriggles, munching on strawberries and cheese . . .

Wait – had it all been a dream? Was I *still* dreaming? I looked around, confused for a moment. Miss Stemper? Bess? Mum and Dad? Where *was* everyone? Was this one of those dreams where you wake up *inside your dream* and you think your dream's over but really you're just in another dream, or another layer of dream?

You must achieve Inlightenment, oh, Legendary Hero!

Hang on a minute. Was it a dream – or was it a *VISION*?

Maybe my Soul had summoned the Spirits of the Living to guide me towards my *hidden truth*? Yes! That must be it. Mum, Dad, Miss Stemper – *they* were the Wise Ancients! Perhaps their dream messages contained the mysterious truth that would lead me to Inlightenment!

Never wear socks with sandals. That couldn't be it. *Sharing is caring.* Didn't seem quite Heroic enough. *Believe and you can do anything . . .* It all seemed a bit vague.

I closed my eyes and focused. *I* was the Hero. It was down to me to seek out my hidden truth. I strained my brain and reached into my Soul until my teeth hurt. When I opened my eyes, I noticed a snowman. It was standing, a little way off, among the other snow shapes I'd built last night.

But this one was different. Its button eyes were staring at me knowingly. Its carroty nose was twitching, like it was trying to tell me something. Had I, with the power of my mind, conjured up a Snow Spirit to guide me towards Inlightenment? I walked cautiously towards it – and suddenly, its twiggy arms fell to the ground and it shook itself alive, in a blizzard of awakening! I braced myself for an intense blast of wisdom. I was ready for Inlightenment!

'I got snow in my pants,' said Olly, jiggling his legs and brushing warm flakes out of his hair. 'Has that copper gone, Harley-arley-arley?'

'Yeah, he's gone,' I sighed.

'D'you like my clever disguise? Not bad, eh? Hey, sorry about pegging it just now, it's just that Sparky got a caution last week and that copper's really got it in for us and . . .' Olly paused for breath, and looked at me with his guilty puppy face. 'I won't run off and leave you again, Harley-arley-arley, I promise. I fully, totally, cross my heart, poke my eyes out, tickle my fancy, *promise* I won't let you down again. I'll be the best Loyal Sidekick you could ever have. I'll –'

'Yeah, whatever,' I said. 'Don't worry about it. I didn't want a sidekick anyway. But now you're here, so let's just . . . get on with it. What about the others, though? What are they going to do?'

'They'll be all right, they got each other,' said Olly. 'They only came along to keep me company.'

'They crawled all that way just to keep you company?'

'Yeah. And they would've crawled all the way back again, if you hadn't come up with that leg-holes idea.'

The thought of Olly's friends crossing the River Betwixt and slithering along a cold rocky path for eight hours just to keep him company . . . It seemed so mad. But then I pictured their happy grinning faces as they'd scrambled up that pylon together, and I figured it had been worth the risk. *A madness, a foolishness, that was worth the risk . . .*

'Come on, Harley-arley-arley! Vroom *vroom VROOM*! Ain't no time for standing round daydreaming – some of us is on the clock! And by some of us, I mean you, seeing as the rest of us is dead. Let's get on with this quest, eh?'

24

7:15 a.m. Friday

2 hours and 45 minutes until Eternal Damnation

Our route back to the Path of Heroes was lined with evil pizzas, singing sweetly and wafting at us. At first, we were strong. Pizza after pizza, we bravely resisted the melty-cheese temptation . . . But there were too many of them. The onslaught continued until we had no choice but to surrender and eat our way back to the Path.

On arrival at the Fourth Task, Olly sat down.

'Too much pizza,' he said. 'Gonna have to sit this one out, I'm afraid.'

'No way,' I said, dragging my stuffed belly over to an

ancient wooden casket. 'You're my sidekick, get up here and get to work.'

Reluctantly, Olly joined me. I unfurled the yellowing parchment that lay beside the casket and read aloud. The ink was so faded that some of the letters had disappeared completely.

> Here Fol ows the F th ask of
> the Leg nd ry Twelv asks.
> ### A Rid le
> Between Sole and Soul
> The Snug Sock Sits:
> **BUT OCKS MUST BE SOR E !**

I put the parchment to one side and opened the casket. It was full of odd socks.

'Buttocks must be sore,' said Olly, stroking his chin thoughtfully. 'Buttocks must be sore . . . Hmmm. Buttocks *MUST* be sore – but why? Why would a sock make your buttocks sore? Soul, sole – clever! Buttocks, buttocks . . . But . . . ocks . . . ocks – *socks*! Socks must be sore . . . sor*ted*! Oy! Oy! Oy! I reckon we have to sort them socks into pairs.'

'Nice one,' I said, having already sorted several pairs while Olly's brain had been ticking over.

Five minutes later, I'd paired up more than forty socks. I glanced over at Olly's pile, and was surprised to see he'd done twice as many. Maybe he was going to be useful after all. I watched him folding a pair together –

'What are you doing!?' I yelled.

'Sorting. What you doing?'

'That's not sorting – you're not matching them up! You're just putting random socks together! You've got to find two the same.'

Olly shrugged, and carried on.

A moment later, all the socks in the casket had been randomly paired, apart from one.

'Why's there one left?' I asked.

'Probably put three in together somewhere,' said Olly. 'Doesn't matter.'

'Course it matters! The whole point of sorting socks –'

I ducked as a raven with a cat's head swooped down and dropped another scroll at my feet. I unfurled it crossly.

Task Complete.

I stared at the words, trying to make sense of what had just happened. We'd done it all wrong: half the socks were odd, some weren't even in pairs – but we'd still passed. The task, apparently, was "complete". I couldn't understand it. The task *wasn't* complete. It was *a job half done*, as my mum would say; *shoddy workmanship,* as my dad would say.

Olly leaned against a rock, spinning his yo-yo.

'One thing I've learned,' he said, 'is never work too hard. Cut corners, that's my advice. Do things quick. Don't do your best, 'cos then you won't have time to relax. Skive whenever you can. Bunk, truant, cheat, sneak, avoid, hide and trick other people into doing things for you. Whatever you don't do today, you can still not do tomorrow –'

'Wait,' I said. 'Look at this.'

I held up the second scroll, which I'd now unrolled to the very bottom.

'Congratulations on passing the Fifth Task,' Olly read. 'What about it?'

'FIFTH Task?' I said. 'Fifth? We missed one! Where's the Fourth?'

'Hmm,' said Olly, scratching his head.

'We'll have to go back!' I said, close to tears, as a pair of greedy Doubts edged into view.

'Maybe we don't need to,' said Olly.

The Doubts backed off, sensing a whiff of Hope in the air as I looked up.

'What do you mean?' I asked.

'Maybe we don't need to go back and do the Fourth Task. Maybe we don't need to do any of them.'

I stared at him. 'What are you talking about?'

'People – mainly adults – are always making stuff up that ain't really *necessary*. Like school, for example. Or the whole *fork in your right hand, knife in your left hand* nonsense.'

'It's the other way round,' I said, though I wasn't really thinking about cutlery. I was thinking – in the madness of panic and desperation – that maybe Olly might be on to something.

'Don't matter which way round,' said Olly. 'That's the point. It don't matter how you eat your cabbage. It's still cabbage. Don't make no difference. Don't mean nothing. We're in a hurry, right? Gotta get to the Fire Exit before you're trapped forever and your heart shrivels up and all that. What if . . . we skip the Tasks?'

'Skip the Tasks?'

'Just go past. Get to the end quicker.'

'But I've got to do the Tasks.'

'Why?'

'Because –'

'What'll happen if you don't?'

'Well, I . . . I'll . . . *we'll* get savaged by a Beast Guardian and hurled *Beneath*.'

'But you already missed the Fourth Task and that didn't happen.'

It would be fair to say that Olly's new plan had blown my mind. I'd never once, in my whole life, considered *not bothering* as an option. Even when I was a "juvenile delinquent" I'd still done my homework, and said please and thank you, and eaten off plates. *Not bothering* was a totally different way of approaching life. Or death.

And it certainly would make things easier. Maybe I just needed to *place my trust* in Olly's skiving theory. Maybe *FEAR* had hidden this unexpected *TRUTH* from me for long enough.

'Okay,' I said. 'Let's do it.'

25

7:26 a.m. FRIDAY

2 hours and 34 minutes
until Eternal Damnation

At the far end of a deserted car park, an enormous tower of rubbish waited beside the bins. The Sixth Task.

'That's a lot of recycling,' I said.

'Yeah,' said Olly. 'Lucky we're not doing it.'

'Hm.'

Since the surprise sock-pairing success, I'd been struggling to get my head round our new plan of not bothering to do the Tasks. What I *hadn't* prepared for was the idea of *not tidying up*. The thought of leaving this big mess to get smellier and yuckier until someone else had to clear it up just felt wrong.

On the other hand, these were exceptional circumstances. A child in danger! A race against time! A matter of life or death! And maybe Olly was right: who would know if we skipped a Task or two?

A huge, terrifying beast stalked out of the shadows. It had antlers like cutlasses, and bloodshot eyes; its claws were serrated like sawblades, and the steam snorted from its scaly nostrils stung the air with the stench of fish paste and stale coffee. The Guardian of the Sixth Task was the scariest monster I'd seen so far. And although it wore a bright yellow tie with red spots, this quirky accessory didn't make it any less frightening. If anything, the novelty tie made it even scarier – like one of those peculiar supply teachers who might SNAP at any moment.

'What *is* that?' I whispered to Olly.

'Dunno, mate. Looks like a mutant-dinosaur-buffalo-supply-teacher . . .?'

The Beast Guardian growled until the earth shook.

'The Sixth Task is not for the faint-hearted!' it bellowed. 'Should ye wish to continue, ye must have the heart of a lion! The cunning of a coyote! The stealth of a panther! The organisational skills of –'

'No thanks, guv'nor, we're in a hurry,' said Olly, strolling past. I froze, gobsmacked, then scuttled to catch up with him, steering Malcolm on a course as wide as possible past the dinosaur-buffalo-supply-teacher.

'Fair enough,' growled the mutant, and went back to its Rubik's Cube.

We walked on.

'Okay,' I said. 'We seemed to get away with that one. But I'm not sure that's going to work every time.'

'It does,' said Olly. 'Trust me. There's always a way to skive.'

Ten minutes later, the Path of Heroes disappeared into an eerie, unlit tunnel. Carved into the rock above the entrance were the words:

**LABYRINTH OF NO RETURN
ENTRANCE ONLY**

Pulling at a loose thread on my hoodie, I began to unravel it. The reel-of-thread-to-find-your-way-out-of-the-labyrinth plan was foolproof: Craemog the Intrepid used it in the Maze of Despair; Hallyria the Unrelenting used it in the Warren of Wretchedness; Bilbamýn the Bold used it in the Spooky Passage; even Theseus from *The Big Book of* –

'Let's just go round,' said Olly.

I paused in the destruction of my hoodie, which was already half a sleeve smaller. My Loyal Sidekick was pointing to an alleyway which appeared to go round the back of the labyrinth. How had I missed that? It was obviously there, now that Olly pointed it out. I guess I just . . . wasn't looking for it. Olly's skiving skills were genuinely impressive. It was like he had a sixth sense for spotting shortcuts.

'Yeah, let's,' I said, tucking the unspooled thread back up my half sleeve.

Eighteen seconds later, we were round the back of the LABYRINTH OF NO RETURN, which presumably tunnelled deep into the cliff. Going in might've cost us hours, or even our Souls. And we'd just slipped by, without bothering to try.

And that was the moment I knew, for almost certain, that this time, I really had . . . *achieved Inlightenment!*

I still wasn't *completely* 100% flying. But I felt really close to . . . maybe not flying exactly, but perhaps . . . almost hovering. Or at least floating. Nearly. If I closed my eyes and *believed*. And after all the misery and disappointment of the last day, that was good enough for me.

The truth that fear had hidden from me was this: the Twelve Tasks were a con. A trick. A distraction from the Legendary Hero's *True* Quest – to escape Death and return to Life.

And it wasn't just the Twelve Tasks either. *All* work was pointless. Errands, jobs, homework, chores: all a waste of time. Suddenly, the foolishness of my past life flashed in front of my eyes. All those mornings hanging out washing – pointless! All those afternoons tidying my room – worthless! All those years at school – wasted!

I shuddered at the thought of where my life might've ended up if I hadn't achieved Inlightenment now. I pictured the Beast Guardian of the Third Task, sobbing in its wonky gallery. That could've been my future. Jobs weren't just a waste of time: they were cruel.

From now on, I must avoid work at all costs. *Not Bothering* – that was the key to success. After all, I hadn't bothered learning the Rites of the Death Master, and look at me now – a True Legendary Hero marching triumphantly along the Path of Heroes! And if I just *placed my trust* in the true wisdom of skiving, then very soon, I would FLY.

Finally, I had discovered the truth that fear had hidden deep within me. And it was all thanks to the fake-imaginary-actually-dead boy with luminous socks. Olly. My Loyal Sidekick.

I marched on with a spring in my step. Armed with Inlightenment, the path felt less treacherous, the trolley less wonky, and the underworld less gloomy.

Guarding the Seventh Task was the Dreaded Polyops of Eastleigh – the most fearsome of all the Dreaded Polyops. Many nights had I quaked behind a cushion as Pops terrified me with tales of this many-eyed monster's ferocity. And here it was in the flesh, looming menacingly between an Epic Mound of Crumpled Washing and a Heroic Ironing Board. The Dreaded Polyops had eyes everywhere. It saw

everything. Some of its eyes looked deep into my Soul; others stared into my future. It kept one eye on the football results, and another eye on the weather forecast. Some of its eyes just looked at its other eyes. But as we passed by without stopping, the Dreaded Polyops of Eastleigh didn't bat a single eyelid.

Beyond the Seventh Task, the underworld brightened up even more. A pink sun sank behind sparkling snow-capped peaks, while a golden sun rose over a glistening dew-soaked meadow. Green hills, awash with daffodils and rainbows and marshmallows, rolled down to a blue lagoon, where butterflies danced between lilies. I felt a warm glow inside; this truly was a world for Heroes.

The Guardian of the Eighth Task was the Swift-Footed Gazellopuss. Judging from its muscular, aerodynamic body, I could easily believe Grandpa's many tales of its legendary speed. But it was sitting behind an Epic Tower of Washing-Up, looking glum. Apparently, the Eighth Task had nothing to do with racing to the death at all. I felt sorry for it. It should've been zooming about, not cooped up behind a load of dirty cups and plates.

The Ninth Task was yet another forgettable household chore – one that may have involved mops, but certainly didn't involve arm-wrestling, despite being supervised by my number one favourite deadly beast of all time. Yes, here it was at last: the Many-Limbed Optimugoon! The hideous creature smiled sadly as we passed. And waved, and waved, and waved . . .

I felt bad for all these miserable monsters. In the stories – *all* the stories – the monsters were constantly being attacked and dying horribly. But somehow, being stuck here, in these dead-end jobs, seemed worse.

'Can I tell you something?' asked Olly, as we strolled on.

'What?'

'From the moment we met, I had a feeling about you, Harley-arley-arley – vroom *vroom VROOM*! I could tell you was special. I think I always knew, deep down, that you would become a Legendary Hero.'

'Really?'

'No, not really. Oy! Oy! Oy! Are you gonna miss me?'

'No,' I said.

'I can't come back with you, you know. I'm stuck here forever, whatever happens.'

'Yep.'

'Mind you, when you've been a Restless Soul for as long as I was, it makes you appreciate being proper dead. All that time *Before*, when my spirit just didn't feel ready to pass *Beyond* –'

'Why wasn't it ready?' I asked, curious to find out more about the unexplained Restlessness of Olly's Soul.

'Eh?' said Olly, looking shifty, like he'd said something he shouldn't have.

'Why did you stay away from the Portal for so long?' I said. 'You know, before you met me.'

'I told you. I just liked being a ghost. It was a laugh.'

Olly got out his yo-yo and fiddled with its string. He seemed reluctant to talk about it, and that made me even curiouser – because Olly *loved* talking, especially about himself.

'But why was your Soul so Restless?' I asked.

'We're all different, I s'pose,' said Olly, fumbling with his yo-yo as a badly launched Swirling Turbo Toss went haywire and spun up his arm. 'One of them psychedelicologists might be able to explain it to you – but they'd have to be dead. And to be honest, most geezers, once they're dead, don't give half a monkey about why this and why that. Most of us prefer to just kick back, enjoy ourselves, forget about the past . . .'

He was hiding something – I was sure of it. Olly knew more about his Soul than he was letting on. Something must've happened, something that stopped him from coming down here for *thirty years*. It was like he'd been trying to avoid something. Or someone.

But before I had a chance to dig any deeper, he vanished.

On the path ahead, I saw what had scared him off.

And it scared me too. I gripped the trolley tightly, my pulse accelerating like a cheetah on rollerskates.

Then I swallowed my panic, held my head high, and carried on walking.

26

7:57 a.m. FRIDAY

2 hours and 3 minutes
until Eternal Damnation

The police officer was examining a moon-buggy parked in front of a NO PARKING sign. One of its wheels had been clamped and it had a parking ticket on the windscreen.

I kept on walking, to avoid drawing attention to me and my brother and our tinsel-pimped trolley – or to Olly, wherever he was hiding. I tried not to speed up. I tried not to slow down.

As we got nearer, I could see for definite that it was the same policeman from earlier – the one who'd chased Olly and his mates off the pylon. I tried not to look at him. I tried not to *not* look at him. I hadn't done anything wrong. I had no reason to be afraid.

'Charlie Tango Delta Foxtrot,' he said, replying to the static buzz of his walkie-talkie. 'Some kind of moon-buggy with lasers and jet propulsion, I reckon. We'll have to tow it; it's causing an obstruction. Roger that, over and out.'

I rolled calmly on, like any normal shopper on her way to the supermarket with her own trolley. I thought about humming to show how casual and relaxed and unsuspicious I was. But it was okay, we were passing the policeman now, he wasn't looking, he was busy with the illegally parked moon-buggy, he had no reason to notice a pair of innocent passers-by –

'Nee-nah! Nee-nah!' squealed Malcolm.

The police officer looked up from his notebook.

'Hello, young man!' he said. 'Good morning, miss!'

'Hello,' I said, trying not to look guilty.

'What are you two doing along here? Dangerous, this path is, you know.'

Just tell the truth. We haven't done anything wrong. It'll all be fine.

'Oh, we're okay, thanks. I'm a . . . Hero.'

'A Hero, are you?' The policeman smiled down at me, as if I was a toddler dressed up as Batman. 'Very good, miss. And what kind of Hero business are you on?'

'I'm rescuing my little brother from Eternal Damnation.'

'Damnation, you say?' The police officer got his notebook out and wrote *dam-nay-tion* really slowly with a tiny blunt pencil. 'I'll keep my eyes peeled for that. Now perhaps you could help me with my current investigation. I'm on the trail of a gang of litterers.'

'Litterers?'

'Fly-tippers. Unlicensed waste-dumpers. Illegal rubbish-chuckers. Six days ago, we received reports about gymnastic equipment being thrown into *Beneath*. Balance beams, parallel bars, rings, mats, trampolines, that sort of thing. Have you seen anything suspicious?'

'No,' I said, honestly. 'But why would someone . . .?'

'The criminal mind,' said the officer, 'doesn't work like yours or mine. Who's to say what motivates a lawbreaker? Violent rage, perhaps? Sadly, *Beneath* is often used as an illegal dumping ground. The Dead treat *Beneath* rather like the Living treat the oceans and outer space, filling them with old toothbrushes and satellites . . .'

He peered into the abyss, thoughtfully.

Looking over the edge was something I spent most of my time trying to avoid, but now I found myself following his gaze into the eerie weirdness. Only a few metres below us, milky clouds churned like a living soup. Occasionally, things bubbled to the surface – fangs, claws, fins, wings – hints of the horrors lurking *Beneath*. Strange things, as mysterious as the chunks in Grimston's Sweet Relish. Nightmarish things, flitting past too rapidly for me to know if I'd really seen them: a giant mosquito with the head of a fox; a crow with beaks at both ends; a shaven squirrel with acorn tattoos, its bushy tail spinning like a propeller.

'Anyway, miss, you'd best be getting on with your quest,' said the officer, snapping out of his reverie. 'But before you go, there is one more matter you may be able to assist with.'

He thrust a crumpled, faded photograph at me.

'Have you seen this boy?'

It was Olly.

'Sorry, no,' I said, wishing I didn't have to lie to the police when I was already so close to Eternal Damnation. He looked at me suspiciously, and I started to panic. Could he tell I was lying? Should I confess? Should I run?

I was about to find out how fast I could sprint with

a trolley, when I suddenly remembered something Miss Delaporte had taught us in Year 5: a method for distracting olden-days police officers and throwing them off the scent.

'Do you have the time, please?' I asked.

'One minute past eight, miss,' he replied, evidently pleased to be so useful. 'The early bird catches the worm. Or should that be, the early Hero succeeds in her quest?' He gave me a friendly smile. 'Or perhaps the early law enforcement officer catches . . .' He glanced again at the photo, and his face crumpled. He seemed about to cry, then shoved the picture back into his pocket, said 'Good day, miss!' and threw himself into the official police business in his notebook.

I grabbed the trolley and rolled on down the path.

Phew! That had been close. Thank goodness for Miss Delaporte. It was such a shame she'd had to retire so suddenly. Some of the kids said she got sacked because of her *unconventional methods*. All I know is that Miss Delaporte was one of the few adults who was properly kind to me during the Bad Times – the *only* one who didn't roll her eyes when I mentioned Olly.

'Oy Oy?' said Malcolm, wriggling around in his seat to try and see where our travelling companion had got to.

'No idea, Maccy,' I said. 'I was wondering that myself.'

Where *was* Olly? And what was the secret of his Soul's Restlessness? And why was this police officer so eager to find him? I had a strange feeling that all these things might be connected.

As we rolled on, I kept hoping Olly would pop out from behind a rock or jump out of a tree or burst through a trapdoor. I really, really wanted him to come back so I could find out what was going on!

Also, I kind of just wanted him to come back.

But he didn't pop out from behind a rock or jump out of a tree or burst through a trapdoor. So I just kept walking, trying to ignore the fact that my sidekick had abandoned me – again.

Gradually, the path narrowed, and we left the brightness and colour behind. A cold mist closed in, and the Resentful Beasts of *Beneath* sounded nearer than ever, their screeches and roars echoing through the gloom. With each corner we turned, the noises grew louder, until the beastly choir of snarlings and growlings gave way to solos of individual resentment: the bitter bleating of a goat who'd spent too many years tied to a post; the hateful sigh of a gecko who'd never been on holiday; the scratching, scratching, scratching of an unforgiving hamster, whose cage had never been quite clean enough . . .

Suddenly, there was a terrible flapping of invisible wings and something brushed against my cheek! – But when I turned, it was gone.

I took a deep breath and rolled on.

Around the next corner, a brick wall blocked the path. There was a door in the wall, but the door was locked. I couldn't go round it. I couldn't go over it. I couldn't go under it.

My phone buzzed with a message.

> Hi Harley r u ok? Dad tried to call yesterday but got cut off. Probably your battery died. So you won't read this!!! Anyway, good luck. c u in a couple of hours. Love mum xxx

Good luck? That was weird.

I put my phone away. Then I looked at the locked door in the brick wall, and I wondered if I'd got this Inlightenment thing quite right. It sure would be useful for the flying to kick in around now. How else was Not Bothering going to get me past this problem?

27

8:06 a.m. Friday

1 hour and 54 minutes
until Eternal Damnation

'If you can guess my ferret's name,' said a hideously twisted man, emerging from the shadows behind me, 'I'll give you the key.'

'Aaagh!' I yelped – because I hadn't been expecting anyone to emerge from the shadows (apart from maybe, hopefully, Olly). And this person who had emerged from the shadows was . . . Well, I didn't know what he was. I studied his nasty, crooked face, but it was too ugly and sinister to look at for long. He was like something from a nightmare.

'Who are you?' I asked.

'Never mind who *I* am,' he replied, in a voice like Hope

being trampled underfoot. 'All *you* need to know is that I'm offering you a deal. Guess my ferret's name, and I'll give you the key to the door.'

'Why?'

'It's a game,' said the twisted man. 'It'll be fun.'

The man's wrinkly skin was hanging from his scrawny arms, and I could see too much of it because he was wearing a vest for a far bigger man.

'Why should I trust you?' I asked.

'Got no choice.'

I looked at the wall. There was definitely no way round it, no way over it . . .

'Where's your ferret now?'

'Not here.'

'I need to see it, so I can make a good guess.'

'Can't. He's at home, sleeping. Went out last night.'

'How many guesses do I get?'

'One.'

'Three's the usual amount.'

'One.'

I stood, thinking. There really wasn't any point guessing the name of a ferret I'd never seen. It could be called anything. Even if I made the one-in-a-million correct guess, this twisted little man could just lie, and say I was wrong.

Then again, like he said: what choice did I have?

'Tell you what,' said the twisted man, 'I'll let you have

three guesses. If you get it wrong, I get your biscuits.'

I looked at the half-empty packet sticking out of my pocket. The Biscuits of Paphiphony! This must be their destiny! I congratulated myself for not eating them – but resisted doing the Victory Shuffle, and calmly agreed to the deal.

'Guess One,' said the twisted man.

'Ferris,' I said, barely hesitating.

The twisted man paused. I'd done it! First time! Boom! Ferris the ferret! What a great name for a ferret! Ferris was the boy out of that film that Olly thought was funny. It was exactly the sort of thing a twisted man on a perilous path Beyond the Back of Beyond would call his pet ferret –

'Wrong,' said the twisted man. 'Guess Two.'

For a moment, I hesitated – then it occurred to me that Heroes don't Hesitate. So I stopped hesitating, apart from that little bit of hesitation while I was thinking about the Heroes don't Hesitate thing – and then another short hesitation while I thought about the fact that thinking about not hesitating had made me hesitate – but at least I wasn't hesitating to think of ferret names, so perhaps it still counted.

'Pammy!' I blurted out.

'Guess Three,' said the twisted man, licking his lips.

Okay, so Not Hesitating wasn't working out.

This time, I decided to Go Fully Mindful.

Going Fully Mindful was another one of the tricks Miss

Delaporte taught us in Year 5, shortly before her surprise retirement. All we had to do was sit in silence until the correct answer appeared in our heads. Usually we'd sit for the whole day and the bell would ring for home time before anyone got it. But that was only because we didn't know what the question was. Right now I did know the question, so Going Fully Mindful was definitely worth a try. I emptied my brain and waited for the ferret's name to float into view from the dark corners of my subconscious.

'The Right Honourable Zebedee Jones, 4th Duke of Biddumshire,' I said, in a tone of blissful calm.

'Incorrect. Biscuits!'

The twisted man held out his twisted hand. Reluctantly, I passed him the chocolate biscuits – but only after taking two and shoving them in my mouth.

The twisted man enjoyed that. It was probably the sort of thing he would've done.

'Another go?' he asked.

'Yes,' I said, confident I was close to guessing the right name.

'This time, if you lose, I get the hoodie.'

'Okay,' I said. 'Ferdie.'

'No.'

'Fergie.'

'No.'

'Himalayan Bob.'

'Close, but not quite. Hoodie!'

Again, the twisted hand. I removed my hoodie – which was covered in the ghostly slime of Doubts and Regrets – and handed it over.

'Come on,' I said, my heart racing from the thrill of my brand-new gambling addiction. 'One more chance.'

'This time,' said the twisted man, stroking his twisted chin, 'we play for the child's toy. If you lose, I get the cuddly lizard. If you win, you get the key.'

I swallowed. *No deal* was clearly the correct answer. I couldn't gamble Diddy Dino! What if I lost? But I couldn't lose, I wouldn't lose . . . This was my chance to win.

'Deal!' I said. I was out of control.

'Ready?' sneered the twisted man.

I looked at Malcolm in his trolley seat, and he looked up at me with his big, expectant eyes. He had his Diddy Dino gripped tightly around the neck, in the usual loving headlock. Whatever happened, I simply could not lose my brother's favourite toy in the whole wide world of the Living and the Dead.

Come on, Harley, you can do this! Just THINK FERRET . . .

'Toothy Tim?'

'Nope.'

'Furry Stanley. . . Oh, I don't know, this is impossible!'

'Last guess,' said the twisted man, grinning like the back of a bin lorry.

'Dada Poo-Poo Bum!' said Malcolm.

The grin widened to reveal a perfect set of rotten gums.

'Congratulations,' said the twisted man, passing me a key.

'Yes!' I yelled, doing the Victory Shuffle, and hugging my genius brother. I put the key in the lock; it fitted. I turned the key; the door unlocked. I grabbed the handle, turned it and opened the door. Then I turned to grab the trolley . . .

And stumbled. My hand was stuck to the door handle. Stuck fast. Like superglue.

I did what any fool would do, and grabbed my stuck hand with my other hand to pull it free. Then that hand was stuck too.

Biscuit crumbs spilled from the edges of the twisted man's crooked grin. He pulled my hoodie on and tried out a few looks. Hood up, hands in pockets, hood down, hands out of pockets. In the end, he settled for tucked in at the waist with the sleeves rolled up.

Then he wheeled the trolley – and my brother – through the door and up the path. I tried desperately to wrench myself free from the super sticky door handle, but it was hopeless. As they disappeared into the darkness, the man's twisted cackle was soon drowned by the sound of Malcolm's screams.

28

8:12 a.m. FRIDAY

1 hour and 48 minutes
until Eternal Damnation

'Oy! Oy! — where's Malcolm?' asked Olly, emerging from some other shadows.

I was on my knees, with my hands stuck to the door handle, cursing under a flock of Regrets.

'He's gone,' I whispered, still struggling to comprehend the enormity of how awful everything had become. 'Kidnapped.'

'*Kidnapped?*'

'You should've been here, Olly!' I snapped, my despair exploding into rage. 'There were creatures *flapping* and . . . *some weird man has taken Malcolm*! You were meant to be helping! What's the point of a sidekick who runs away at the first sign of trouble?'

'Yeah, sorry, I . . . Look, why don't you just let go of the door, and I'll explain –'

'I can't let go, I'm *STUCK*!!!'

'You what? Hold on a minute.' Olly grabbed my arms and pulled. 'You're stuck.'

'Thanks, Loyal Sidekick, that's a great help. Now, can you please help me get *un*stuck?'

'Oh right, yeah,' said Olly. 'Great plan, Legendary Hero!'

He examined my hands and the door handle, thoughtfully.

'Or,' he said, 'I could go and get Malcolm back. Which way did he go?'

'The creepy demon thing wheeled him through the door and down the path.'

'Creepy demon, you say? Right. Okay. Don't worry, Harley-arley-arley! You just wait here.'

Olly knelt down to tie his shoelaces.

'So, er, this demon,' he said, staring at his feet as he fiddled with his trainers. 'How creepy are we talking? Like, *proper* creepy? Or just a *bit* cree—'

Suddenly, before Olly could put off being brave any longer, a woman in a golden leotard cartwheeled gracefully through the open door and landed neatly beside us. I looked up at her – and then I couldn't stop looking, because she was the most perfectly beautiful person I'd ever seen. She was so perfectly beautiful that, for a moment, I almost forgot the horrifying nightmare I was living through. She stood, very straight and very still, her perfect arms pointing directly heavenwards, towards my salvation. Then she smiled, and I thought she really must be an angel, come to save me at the moment of my deepest despair.

'Did my husband do that?' she asked, nodding towards the door handle. 'Little man. Big vest. Very ugly.'

'Your husband?' I gasped. 'That man is *your husband*?'

The idea that anyone could've married that nasty, twisted man was shocking enough – but someone as perfect and lovely as this?

'Your husband stole my brother!' I said.

'Doesn't surprise me,' said the beautiful gymnast. 'He's a terrible person. Catch you out with the sticky-handle trick, did he? Don't worry, you just need some of that special soap from the Heroic Toilets.'

'Heroic Toilets?' I said. 'I didn't notice any –'

'Very badly signposted,' she said, doing the splits. 'A lot of people miss them, but they're all along the Path of Heroes, every kilometre or so. Health and Safety requirement. Nearest ones are just around the corner. When you come to a yellowish-grey rock next to a pinkish-grey rock, look for a tiny crevice in the cliff – squeeze through and you'll find the loos. Your sidekick can pop along and fetch you some soap and you can grease yourself free.'

'Me?' said Olly, grinning stupidly. 'How did you know I was her sidekick?'

'Just a guess,' said the gymnast, doing a handstand.

I couldn't help smiling at that. If this amazing and beautiful person had guessed Olly was my sidekick, then she must've guessed I was a Hero! Then I thought of Malcolm's frightened little face, and I felt pretty stupid and pathetic for feeling pleased with myself. Some Hero I was.

'Anyway, I can't stop,' said the woman, bending over backwards. 'I'm going back to the Back of Beyond, and it's a long way to cartwheel.'

'I know a song that can help you pass the time,' said Olly, gleefully.

'No, Olly, please!' I begged, trying desperately to pull myself loose so I could stop him from embarrassing everyone – but it was too late.

> *'Oy! Oy! Oy! Bish bash bosh!*
> *Ding dong dang! Gilly gilly gosh!*
> *We're going to the back to the back to the back*
> *We're off to the Back of Beyond! OY!'*

'I like that!' said the woman. *'Oy! Oy! Oy!'*
'Try liking it after an hour,' I muttered.

'Oliver Polliver, at your service,' said Olly, bowing and curtseying and saluting. 'Composer, entertainer, yo-yo master and Loyal Sidekick to the Legendary Hero, Harley Lenton – among other things.'

'Pleased to meet you, Oliver and Harley. I'm Lovelia.'

'Lovelier than what?' I asked, wondering if she'd be modest enough not to say *everything* – even though that was probably the correct answer.

'No, Lovelia's her *name*,' said Olly. 'Like that woman last week – you know, the beautiful gymnast who died too soon, cartwheeling down the motorway for charity? The one who was getting rescued by Idolic— *Hang on a minute! You're* a beautiful cartwheeling gymnast. You're not . . . she was . . . are you . . . Is it *you*? The beautiful cartwheeling gymnast who died too soon and made the whole internet sad? The one who was getting rescued by Idolicles?'

'Ha!' said Lovelia, with a look of disgust at the mention of Idolicles that made her suddenly a bit less lovelier.

'But that twisted demon thing who took Malcolm wasn't Idolicles,' I said. 'He couldn't have been. Idolicles is a Classic Hero! He's brave and muscly and clever and handsome . . . Everyone says so!'

'Yeah, Idolicles is *famous* for being big and brave and strong!' said Olly.

'Ha!' said Lovelia. 'And just look at him now!'

'You mean, that twisted man who took Malcolm really *was* Brave Idolicles?'

'Ha!' said Lovelia again. 'Let me give you some advice, kids. Never get married! Marrying that man was the worst thing I ever did.'

'Worse than cartwheeling down a motorway?' Olly asked.

'Yes!' said Lovelia. 'I didn't even *want* to be rescued. I *liked* being dead. Oh, I was perfectly fine, somersaulting through the Happy Meadow – until *he* came along and decided to "save" me. Drove me along this stupid path in his stupid Heroic moon-buggy. I kept telling him I didn't even *want* to go back up, but he was determined to have his GLORY, *desperate* to be the Big Man Hero . . . And now look at him! Shrivelled heart, twisted spine, bent fingers, crooked liver . . .'

'And that's *why* he's all shrunken and shrivelled and twisted – because he *failed*?'

Lovelia nodded, smiling miserably. 'We didn't make it to the Fire Exit in time, and now he's an Official Failure! But you'd better find him, because it sounds to me like that vain fool is planning to rescue your brother, in a desperate final attempt to become a True Legendary Hero. And believe me, being rescued by Idolicles is a very unpleasant affair!'

And with that, she cartwheeled away, singing,

'*Oy! Oy! Oy! Bish bash bosh!*' as she twirled into the swirling mists.

'I'll get that soap!' said Olly, half attempting a cartwheel, then thinking better of it and sauntering off to the Heroic Toilets.

And I was left alone, stuck to a door handle, to think.

And even though I was alone and stuck to a door handle, I felt more determined than ever. Failure was not an option! Not that it ever had been. I just hoped Olly would hurry up with that soap and avoid getting distracted by a pylon or playing with his yo-yo or chatting to a monster or singing about *gilly gilly gosh* or hiding from the police or any of the other bazillion things that could easily distract him.

I thought about that smarmy interviewer and the kiosk man and all those picnickers who'd been so sure of Idolicles' success. Yet he'd failed – *officially* – and they had no idea. "Brave Handsome Idolicles" was a twisted child snatcher. But back at the Happy Meadow, everyone was still talking about him like he was one of those Classic Heroes in the paintings.

Then again, what if *those* Heroes weren't really what they seemed to be either? What if they didn't really slay all those monsters? What if, really, they just Heroically did some chores and DIY? What if they were faking it? Faking it for the paintings, and the movies, and the stories?

And if they *were* all faking it, then maybe it was time for those Fake Old Classic Heroes to step aside and make way for a New Modern Hero! But probably not one that got stuck in fences and glued to door handles and couldn't be trusted to look after her little brother.

29

8:21 a.m. FRIDAY

1 hour and 39 minutes
until Eternal Damnation

'*Eyore!*'

Olly was back, and he was riding on a donkey.

'I got the special soap,' he said, dismounting.

'Thanks,' I said. 'You were surprisingly quick.'

'Yeah, well – I got me a trusty donkey.'

He poured a plimsoll-ful of greasy liquid soap over my hands. I wriggled my fingers and eventually they slipped free.

'Eugh,' I said. 'That's gross. But, you know, thanks.'

Olly put his plimsoll back on.

'So, where did you get the donkey?' I asked.

The donkey was wearing a battered straw hat and looked depressed, but that might've just been his normal donkey expression.

'Told you I could Summon the Beasts, didn't I?' said Olly.

'Yeah,' I said. 'But where did you get the donkey?'

'I *summoned* it!'

'Right,' I said. 'Summoned as in *stole* or *found*?'

'Whoa there!' said Olly – to me, not the donkey. 'That's out of order, Harley-arley-arley! I just proper *saved* you – and I done it quick – and my shoe's gonna be proper squelchy for a long time. So a bit of *Well done, Loyal Sidekick* wouldn't go amiss right now.'

'Yeah, sorry,' I said. 'Well done, Loyal Sidekick. I'm sorry for doubting your Beast-Summoning skills. And I really do appreciate you getting the greasy soap for me, even though carrying it in your shoe was gross.'

We walked on down the path.

'So where did you find the donkey?'

'He was just hanging around outside the toilets,' said Olly. 'I reckon he's one of them Resentful Beasts from *Beneath* – probably did rides on the beach, you know, one of them sad, exploited donkeys. But I reckon he's come *up* from *Beneath* because maybe it's *too* resentful for animals like him down there. I don't think donkeys are so into revenge as, like, sharks and alligators. Anyway, I didn't *find* him, I *summoned* him, remember – with my powers.'

'Yeah, okay,' I said, smiling.

We rounded another bend and stopped in front of a cosy-looking wooden cabin with smoke puffing peacefully out the chimney. A sign above the door said:

MISERY AT LAST

REST HOME FOR FAILED HEROES

'Do you reckon Idolicles might be in here?' I said.

'Worth a try,' said Olly.

As I approached, I wished I had my rolled-up *Risborough Gazette*. I knew a local newspaper wasn't really going to help in a battle with the undead, but I'd kind of got used to the idea that it meant something.

I pushed open the door, and a terrible stench wafted over us.

'Bleeurrghh!' I said.

'Yeooweurgh!' said Olly.

It was a stale, dry-damp, musty smell. Worse than the purgatorial smoke after the Portal of Doom slammed shut in the caravan. Worse than that expensive cheese Dad buys at Christmas. Worse than Olly's plimsoll (the one without soap in it).

We pulled our T-shirts up over our noses and bravely peeped round the open door. Like the TARDIS, the REST HOME FOR FAILED HEROES was bigger on the inside. Much bigger. Through a dim haze of despair, I could see hundreds of old Failed Heroes, slumped on worn-out armchairs – but there could've been a million or more, because the far end of the cabin stretched away to the horizon, with doors and corridors leading off in every direction.

The Failed Heroes sat around in varying states of shrivelled twistedness. Some were being hugged into a deeper misery by piles of knobbly Regrets, flopped over their laps like blubbery blankets, or feeding off their feet like parasitic slippers. But most of these Failed Heroes had nothing left on them for the Regrets to take. Many were little more than skeletons, whose jawbones creaked as their skulls chattered away, moaning and whining and boasting and arguing.

'This lot could do with a sing-song,' said Olly.

'Or at least a telly,' I suggested.

I peered through the dim haze of misery – and suddenly, way off in the distance, beyond at least a hundred moaning half skeletons, a trolley rattled by.

'It's him!' I yelled. Idolicles turned to look at us, a half-munched biscuit spilling from his open mouth. He cackled, shoved another of the celebrated Biscuits of Paphiphony into his gnarly gob, and skittered away.

'Maccy!' I shouted, rushing after them, dodging between Failed Heroes and jumping over bony feet on tattered footstools. But before I could reach them, Noble Idolicles the Child Snatcher turned a corner and disappeared down a maze of corridors. I skidded to a stop, unsure which way to go.

'Crumbs!' gasped Olly, when he and his slow-trotting donkey caught up. I followed my sidekick's eagle-eyed gaze to the floor, where a few tiny biscuit crumbs lay in a row.

'Gotcha!' I said, confident that this biscuity trail would lead us to the kidnapper – just like the trail of berries that led Mibble and Frifenella to their destiny at the far side of the Inevitable Forest.

We followed the crumbs down corridors and across

rooms full of Failed Heroes in armchairs and through doors and down more corridors . . .

'Look, Harley-arley-arley!' said Olly. 'It's the Tunic of Qu'architi-Nu!'

Grabbing my hoodie off the floor, I felt a rush of hope. Idolicles had been wearing it – which meant he must be getting hot – which meant he was probably getting tired – which meant we were probably catching him up! I ran even faster – left, right, right, left, left, left, right . . .

'Aaaaghhh!' I yelled, crashing into the policeman. 'Olly! I haven't found Oll— The boy, I haven't found the boy you're looking for, officer!'

Olly must've heard my warning and hung back, keeping himself and his donkey out of sight.

The police officer looked at me suspiciously.

'So you haven't seen Olly?'

'No, I haven't seen him – I mean, who's Olly? I'm guessing that's the name of the boy you're searching for?'

'You said his name!'

'Only because you did.'

'No! You said it first! You *know* him! You're *hiding* him! I could arrest you, young lady, for harbouring a known felon! I've half a mind to!'

'But I'm a Legendary Hero on a Noble Quest! You'd be obstructing the course of justice!'

'No, *you're* obstructing the course of justice! I *am*

justice, remember? I am the *law*! Anyway, I'm just trying to find my boy . . . I mean, *a* boy.'

'Yeah, well I'm on the trail of a child snatcher!'

I looked at the crumb trail trickling away behind him. I didn't have time for this.

'Child snatcher, eh?' The policeman took out his notebook and wrote very slowly with his blunt pencil. '*Child. Snatch. Er. I. Dent. If. Ied. In. Rest. Home . . .*'

By the time he'd completed the sentence, I was three corridors away.

I followed the crumb trail around two more corners and ran into Olly.

'Olly!' I whispered. 'That policeman – he's –'

'Not now!' he whispered back. 'Let's find your brother. Come on!'

We went on together, up and down corridors and in and out of lounges full of decaying Failed Heroes – until the trail of crumbs ended. And there, on the threadbare carpet, was a sock. A tiny sock covered in multicoloured dinosaurs. A sad, solitary sock, separated from a small, cold foot.

'We've got that nasty demon now!' said Olly, holding Malcolm's sock up to the donkey's quivering nostrils.

'*Eey*ore!' said the donkey.

'What are you doing?' I asked. 'Is he . . . a sniffer donkey?'

Olly nodded and closed his eyes.

'Oy! Oy! Oy! Lord Donkey!' he said, in a loud sort of wizard voice. 'WHAT WAY IS MALCOLM, PLEEEEEEASE?'

The donkey stuck its nose in the air, and a look of intense concentration came over its long, bristly face. Closing its eyes in deep meditation, it tensed and strained and shuddered . . .

FLUMP. THR-RR-OOPFF. PLUMF.

'Interesting,' said Olly, as he thoughtfully examined the smelly pile of wisdom the donkey had offered from its rear. After a moment he stepped back, to consider the creature's steaming advice from a more comfortable distance.

'Let's try this way,' he said, walking away from the smell.

'You can't just leave that there!' I said. 'You need to clean up after your pet. Haven't you got one of those bags like dogwalkers use?'

'I'm afraid not, Harley-arley-arley. Don't forget, I'm from the past. In the 1980s, no one carried poo around in bags. We had more dignity.'

Well, there wasn't time to argue my point now, because I'd suddenly noticed a warm glow spilling from an open door ahead. I hurried along the corridor and looked inside.

This room was different to the others we'd passed through. It was smaller and cosier, and it was *empty* – not a single Failed Hero in sight. It was still full of armchairs, but these armchairs were new, and each one had a notice on it.

RESERVED FOR GORMON
THE GREAT FAILED HERO

RESERVED FOR LILLIUNA
THE LAZY FAILED HERO

RESERVED FOR FANFOSCARELLI
THE FABULOUS FAILED HERO

Were these chairs reserved for future Failed Heroes? That was so unfair! What if they *didn't* fail? Weren't they given a chance? Was this their destiny, before they'd even set off?

'Eeyore!' said the donkey, sniffing a flowery-patterned chair.

RESERVED FOR NOBLE IDOLICLES
THE FAILED CHILD SNATCHER

Failed child snatcher. Did this mean . . .?

'Yes!' I shouted, pumping my fist in the air and doing the Victory Shuffle – not even caring that Olly could see my secret dance. We were going to get Malcolm back! Idolicles would fail again! Destiny was on our side! Everything was going to be okay!

'Right, let's go!' said Olly. I turned around to see him jiggling about in front of a chair, looking shifty. 'Nothing more to see here. Let's crack on, eh?'

'Why are you acting weird?' I asked.

'I'm not,' said Olly, weirdly. 'Oh look, there's the door.'

I tried to look at the chair behind him and he dodged about, blocking my view.

'Fine, let's go,' I said, stepping towards the door – but as soon as he followed, I darted behind him and read the chair notice he'd been hiding.

PHLOOOMP!

The Doubts pounced. Darkness. Silence.

It was all over.

The End.

RESERVED FOR HOPELESS HARLEY
THE LEGENDARY FAILED HERO

30

8:37 a.m. FRIDAY

1 hour and 23 minutes until Eternal Damnation

A sliver of dull light broke through as Olly peeled back a tentacle.

'Oy! Oy! Oy!' he said, gently.

I groaned. It wasn't all over. I wasn't dead. Just crushed by a fresh crop of Doubts and Regrets. Olly was probably going to drag me over a hill again, but I couldn't even bring myself to care.

'All I had to do was look after Maccy,' I despaired. 'Why've I never got any good news to tell my parents? How do I manage to keep letting them down all the time?'

'Oh no, no, no!' said Olly, shaking his head vigorously. 'Don't start that. Listen, Harley-arley-arley, I'm gonna tell you a story. Are you lying comfortably?'

I raised an eyebrow. I was crushed against a smelly old carpet by a ton of pulsating blubbery parasites.

'Then I'll begin,' Olly continued. 'You wanna know about letting parents down? I wrote the book on it, mate! Not literally, of course. I would never *literally* write a book. I'm not an idiot. Anyway, I *really* let my dad down, like, way more than you could ever dream of. He proper hates me. And you can't even blame him, after what I done.'

I tried, unsuccessfully, to flick another tentacle out of my other eye.

'That policeman,' I said.

'Oh,' said Olly. 'Yeah. When did you work it out?'

'He kind of let it slip, just now. But I knew he seemed familiar, and for ages I couldn't place it, but . . . He looks like you.'

'You reckon?'

'Sort of.'

'Yeah, well. My old man became a copper – a police officer – 'cos he really likes rules. He *loves* rules! And safety, and notebooks. It ain't natural, I'm telling you. I *hate* rules! Sometimes I don't even believe he *is* my dad. But I still wanted to please him *all the time*. Everything I did annoyed him, but I didn't *want* to annoy him. I wanted to make him proud . . .'

Olly stared at the peeling wallpaper.

'One day, I luzzed my Frisbee and it got stuck in a pylon. So I climbed up the pylon, just like them TV adverts told us not to. My dad sees me, shouts at me to stop. I get frightened – I'm stuck. Can't climb down. So he climbs up to get me . . . *BOOM!* Hundred thousand volts through both of us. Bish bash bosh – I'm dead, he's dead. We're both dead.'

A few Regrets peeled themselves off my back and squelched on to Olly. I felt bad for feeling so sorry for myself.

'Now obviously my dad hates me for this. My mum probably hates me even more – I killed her kid *and* her husband. So I ran away. I stayed up there, hiding in *Before*, and avoided coming down here so I didn't have to face him. I steered clear of BK and wandered about as a Restless Soul, messing about, for thirty years! That's how I got to know your grandparents and become friends with you.'

'He doesn't hate you,' I said.

'Yeah, yeah, blah, blah. He does and he should. Don't give me all your slushy social worker guff about it – he's angry and he wants to arrest me to teach me a lesson. Reckons a few nights in a police cell will sort me out. And

I *know* this, 'cos when I finally come down last Christmas, he meets me! *He's* my Guide! Through the field of Nothingness, down the beige road, up the escalator. And the whole way along, he don't say a word to me. So as soon as we get to the Back of Beyond, I leg it. He chases me with his stupid whistle – and that's how it's been ever since.'

He picked at a loose thread on a nearby armchair.

'Anyway, the point is, sometimes you can't be what your mum and dad want you to be. That's just how it is.'

I lay still, wondering how to persuade Olly he might be wrong about his dad.

'Look, thanks for lying for me. You really are a proper mate, Harley-arley-arley. But I gotta be honest: right now, we ain't got time for all this lounging about, feeling sorry for ourselves. We gotta get on with it.'

'But what's the point if I'm destined to fail?'

'Fail? You? What a load of nonsense! *You* are a Legendary Hero, Harley Lenton. Trust me, armchairs are always wrong about this sort of thing. Now come on, you pillock! Let's get out of here.'

The remaining Doubts heaved a blubbery sigh and slunk off. I had a feeling they were learning something I'd known for years: Oliver Polliver was nothing but trouble.

We stepped back into the corridor and I noticed a door with a NO EXIT sign. I barged through it and stumbled on to the Path of Heroes – to be confronted with a sight more terrifying than any monster, and more impassable than any wall.

It was Idolicles, holding Malcolm by the ankles and dangling him head first above the icy darkness of *Beneath*.

31

8:43 a.m. FRIDAY

1 hour and 17 minutes
until Eternal Damnation

'Maccy!' I called, reaching out – but when I stepped towards him, Idolicles let go of one of his legs.

'One step closer, and I drop the babby!' he snarled.

I froze as Malcolm's bewildered face peered into the swirling mists.

'Arwee?' he whimpered.

'It's okay, Maccy!' I said. 'It's going to be okay. I'm going to sort this out.'

'Shhh!' said Idolicles, raising a crooked finger to his lips. 'Shhh.'

Then he sang, swinging Malcolm over the abyss as the

tortured melody scratched its way out of his throat like a rat escaping from a violin.

> *'Hush little baby, don't you cry,*
> *Idolicles the Failed Legendary Hero's gonna*
> *sing you a lullaby,*
> *And if all the lines don't fit exactly right or*
> *rhyme properly,*
> *You're just going to put up with it because*
> *otherwise I'll drop you.'*

At the end of the verse, Idolicles paused and sniffed the air hungrily. Slowly, a thin, cruel tongue slithered down his chin, searching out a soggy biscuit crumb that was clinging to a patch of stubble. He slurped up the surprise snack and grinned horribly. Biscuity drool seeped from the edges of his wonky mouth and drip, drip, dripped on to his enormous, filthy vest.

'So we meet again, Harley Lenton,' declared Idolicles the Failed Legendary Hero. 'The chase is over, and now it is time for you and me . . . to come to an arrangement.'

'Okay, just please don't drop him!' I begged. 'I'll do whatever you say, just *please* –'

'Correct, Harley Lenton. You *will* do whatever I say. Because if you don't, I shall fling the child over the edge – to be eternally gobbled and gargled by the Resentful

Beasts of *Beneath*!'

As he spoke, a gobbet of biscuity spittle flew out of his mouth, landing on the path between us.

'Of course, none of us wanted it to be like this,' Idolicles continued. 'I had intended to rescue my wife, the fair Lovelia! And I would have, if it weren't for her ridiculous modern ideas about not wanting to be rescued. Oh, she put up such a fight, flinging her gym equipment at me and trying to cartwheel away! It's her fault we didn't reach the Fire Exit in time. I bravely completed the Twelve Tasks, but *she* made us late! Well, her and that infernal parking ticket.'

Idolicles held Malcolm in front of his face, staring at him like a snake sizing up its prey.

'Look at you, little frowning babby! It would've meant greater glory for me if you were the most beautiful celebrity cartwheeler of the millennium. But at least you won't nag, nag, nag, with all your endless opinions.'

'So is this your plan?' I asked. 'To "rescue" Malcolm for another shot at the glory you always dreamed of?'

'*Ha!* Too late for that! Too late for that gorgeous, handsome, muscular fellow who used to stare at me so lovingly from the mirror . . . He's gone. Yes, it's too late for him!'

From the corner of my eye, I spotted Olly and his donkey sneaking into the shadows behind us while Idolicles ranted on. My twisted nemesis was so caught up in his supervillain monologue, he didn't seem to have noticed my sidekick at all.

'Alas, poor Idolicles!' said Idolicles. 'Alas, Brave Idolicles the Nearly-Champion! Oh, he really should have become a Legendary Hero – he certainly had the looks for it.'

'So, what *do* you want Malcolm for, if it's already too late for "Poor Idolicles"?' I asked.

Idolicles grinned nastily. 'Oh, *Malcolm*! Such a lovely name. Little Malcolm, my cutesy-wutesy little brother . . .'

'Your WHAT?'

'Idolicles is no more!' declared Idolicles, mournfully. 'His comfy chair awaits him! Yes, it's too late for him. But it's not too late for *me*: Harley Lenton the Legendary Hero!'

So *this* was his cunning plan. To steal my identity, just like he'd stolen my biscuits and my hoodie. To pass through the Fire Exit pretending to be me – rescuing *my* brother! It was ridiculous.

'That's ridiculous,' I said. 'No one's going to fall for that.'

'Well, we'll see, won't we?' he replied, scratching himself. 'But I'd recommend you play along, Harley Lenton. It's a good deal for you, with your silly *big heart.* You'll miss out on the glory, and you'll suffer an eternity of shrivelled misery in the Home for Failed Heroes . . . but you'll save your little brother. And that's what you came down here for, isn't it? Little Malcolm will be saved, and you can feel good about yourself.'

'You're mad!'

'Mwah-ha-ha-ha!' laughed Idolicles, madly. 'Now what's it going to be? Are you going to back off and let *me* be Harley Lenton the Legendary Hero? Or shall I hurl this infant *Beneath*? Actually, that does sound rather fun . . . Here's a thought – why don't I drop the boy into the abyss, and you and I join forces as an Evil Duo? We can work together *against* all future Heroes! We can bother them and get in their way, so that *they* FAIL – just like us!'

Malcolm was swinging wildly as each crazy new idea popped into his kidnapper's addled brain. But he was doing his best to enjoy the ride, now that he'd got over the initial shock, cheerfully swooping Diddy Dino above the swirling mists of *Beneath*.

'Sure, you might hate me at first,' Idolicles went on, lost in his mad fantasy, 'but once your heart shrivels and your brain turns to mush, you'll soon start to enjoy yourself. Let's be Legendary *Villains*, Harley Lenton – and all the new stories and legends will be about us! Just think: if I'm this twisted and shrivelled after only one week, imagine what we'll be like in a year! Imagine how *nasty* we'll be then! And what about a hundred years? Or a million? And even after a trillion years of shrivelling and decaying and twisting up, we still won't have got started. Because we're here for *Eternity*!'

Okay, I needed a plan. It was no good talking to this

maniac, and Malcolm might fall at any moment. I started to panic. I felt sick.

But wait. What was this?

Olly? *OLLY!*

Oliver Polliver, my Loyal Sidekick, galloping courageously past me on his donkey, like a knight in shining armour. One arm outstretched, ready to reach out and grab Malcolm, as his trusty steed charged at Idolicles . . .

. . . who stepped aside. The donkey skidded to a halt at the cliff edge, and Olly flew off, soared through the air, then plummeted towards the horrors of *Beneath*.

I ran to the edge and peered over. Olly was nowhere to be seen.

'Your sidekick, I presume?' said Idolicles. 'Well, that's the end of him.'

'Eeyore,' said the donkey, trotting guiltily away.

I stared into the abyss, feeling empty.

'Here's a new proposition for you,' said Idolicles. 'I won't drop the babby if you make ME your new sidekick.'

I looked up at him in disbelief.

'Come on,' said Idolicles, dangling Malcolm wildly. 'What's it going to be? Drop the babby, or new sidekick?'

I stared into the Failed Hero's twisted eyes, those deep pools of cruelty and fear.

'No deal,' I said, and leapt into the abyss.

32

8:54 a.m. FRIDAY

1 hour and 6 minutes
until Eternal Damnation

My plan, roughly, was to fly. Swoop down and rescue Olly, swoop up and grab Malcolm, then swoop along the path to the Fire Exit, without any more bother from Idolicles. I wondered if, up to now, I hadn't taken a big enough *risk* for full Inlightenment to kick in. Maybe I hadn't done enough *believing* for my Body to become lighter than my Soul. After all, Gran and Nana did say it would be risky, mad, foolish and dangerous – and you couldn't get much more risky, mad, foolish and dangerous than jumping into an abyss. This leap would prove how much faith I had in the *truth that fear had hidden from me* – how much I trusted the wisdom of Not Bothering. As long as I *believed*, I'd soon be soaring like an eagle.

It was a long shot, and if I'm honest, I didn't entirely expect it to work. But I had to try something. I couldn't leave Olly *Beneath*.

So far, I was still falling. Plummeting at breakneck speed through a filthy haze of resentment and misery. It felt like being dropped into a cloud of tears, but colder and damper and sadder. As I fell, glimpses of those horrible weird creatures flashed past my eyes – strange, shadowy things with snapping jaws, and slashing claws, and deplorable manners . . .

Down, down, down, through icy swirling mists which eventually thinned enough for me to see the side of the abyss. It was too smooth and damp to grab on to, even if I could've reached. Occasionally, I passed vengeful trees growing out of the rock, rustling their leaves angrily as they poked me with twiggy fingers.

I closed my eyes, to concentrate on the believing.

I'm flying . . . I'm flying . . . I'm flying! – I'm FLYING!

Opened my eyes.

Nope, still falling.

Falling, falling, falling, and beginning to think that I probably shouldn't have jumped. After Olly's pep-talk, I'd felt so inspired, so empowered, so confident – I felt like I could take control of my own destiny and defeat my nemesis. I felt like I could fly! But of course this was one of the classic

Dangers of Friendship – getting all *motivated* and *inspired* to do stuff you really shouldn't be doing. Like melting your mum's shoes, or jumping off a cliff . . .

I was still falling.

Still not floating, still not flying, still not swooping.

So far, this leap of faith was a complete disaster – but until I reached the bottom, there was always Hope.

I tried believing . . . one . . . more . . . time . . .

Then I gave up on that and tried flapping my arms. That didn't work either.

I was just about to use my hoodie as a parachute when the mists cleared, and I saw *Beneath*.

As the ground flew towards me, I felt my senses quicken. Suddenly, I had the superfast reactions of a python lunging at its prey, or a fly dodging a swatting slipper. It felt like everything was happening in slow motion. Was this some kind of Hero Magic? A superpower?

Then I remembered what Pops had said, about time slowing down *Beneath* to make the eternity of suffering last longer. Okay, so the slo-mo wasn't magic or super. It was just a fancy special effect in this *actual* nightmare.

Unsurprisingly, *Beneath* did not look welcoming. Jagged rocks, bubbling lava, snapping crocodiles, stinging nettles, electrified spikes, a trampoline . . .

Wait! A trampoline! I was saved! It must've been Lovelia's, chucked over the edge when she was escaping from Idolicles. Yes! A little further off I could see a broken balance beam, but the trampoline had landed on its feet, and it looked fine. If I could just move towards it . . .

I tried swimming through the air in my slo-mo freefall, but it was like wading through treacle. I was creeping towards the trampoline, but too slowly. The ground was getting bigger, and the details were getting sharper: the shining spikes, the gnashing jaws, the steaming lava, the slow-moving trampoline . . .

The trampoline was moving.

Someone was pushing the trampoline.

Olly was pushing it! Olly was pushing it towards where I was going to land!

But he wasn't alone. Something enormous and prehistoric was following him. Big head, big teeth, tiny arms – Olly was being hunted by a T-Rex! The Tyrant King of the Death Lizards was striding after him, grinding its slavering jaws. Even in slow motion, it moved quickly. Already it was less than a hundred metres away from tearing Olly limb from limb.

I swam as fast as I could, as Olly pushed with all his might. In ultra-slow motion, I flapped and pointed as I fell, trying to warn him about the approaching Death Lizard. Olly smiled, and gave me a thumbs up. I waved my arms, shook my head, and called out – but my shouts came out in that deep, lumpy slo-mo noise that could've meant anything.

When Olly finally looked round, the T-Rex was only a few metres away. He pushed the trampoline another few steps, got it in just the right place, then ran away – very, very slowly. His little legs were no match for the striding predator. But before I could see him being savaged, I landed on the trampoline. The springs stretched, taking me down, down, down, until the mat nearly touched the ground . . .

BOI-OI-OI-OING!

Slow motion ended as I rocketed upwards, leaving *Beneath* below. Up, up, up I flew – like a bird, a plane, a superhero! – until the bounce ran out of momentum, and I landed smoothly on the Path of Heroes.

Idolicles gawped at me. As far as he was concerned, I'd just properly flown here, and landed next to my trolley like a real superhero from an actual movie. And I had, hadn't I? More or less. I'd rocketed upwards – *I'd flown!* I stood with my hands on my hips and my head held high, enjoying this near-enough-heroic moment . . .

But I couldn't shake the image of that slavering T-Rex from my head.

Of course, I knew Olly would be okay. Olly was always okay. Olly got away with *everything*. He'd escape, sneak off, talk his way out of it . . .

Wouldn't he?

I tried to make myself believe. Somehow, he'd nip out the way of the T-Rex's slobbering jaws. Somehow, he'd escape *Beneath*. He wasn't the Heroic Martyr type. Martyrs had to hope that other people bragged on their behalf – Olly would never rely on other people to do his boasting for him.

He'd find a way.

Wouldn't he?

A slippery Doubt seized its moment and flumped quietly round my ankle.

Olly had risked everything to try and save Malcolm. Then he'd risked everything again to save me. I *had* to get him back! And suddenly, quietly, like an unexpected gift, an inkling of a plan tiptoed into my mind. Not a crazy leaping plan, either: a *sensible* plan.

But before I could do anything about Olly, I needed to focus on the situation in front of me. Idolicles was still staring at me, his mouth hanging open. I'd caught him in the middle of taunting Malcolm – holding Diddy Dino just out of reach, while my brother sat on the ground, crying. But Malcolm had stopped crying now. And as I struggled to enjoy my moment of Almost-Heroism, I witnessed some *actual magic.*

Yes. On the ground beside Idolicles – unseen by my gawping nemesis – something wonderful was happening. *Malcolm was taking his first steps!* Quick as a flash, I whipped out my phone. If I missed this, Mum would kill me!

Idolicles posed for the video, unaware that beside him a baby was becoming a toddler. One step . . . two steps . . . three steps . . .

Malcolm snatched Diddy Dino from his kidnapper's twisted hand and stumbled on to his kidnapper's twisted knees, knocking him off balance. Idolicles lurched forward, tripped – and toppled over the precipice into *Beneath.* From where he disappeared into the mist, I reckoned he would've landed just a few metres wide of his wife's trampoline.

'You little legend!' I whooped, grabbing Malcolm and twirling him round in a great big hug.

'Wheeee!' said Malcolm, gleefully flying Diddy Dino into a ferocious cuddle.

As I strapped my brother and his dinosaur back into their trolley seat, I had a feeling everything might be okay after all. Me and Malcolm were back together, we'd vanquished the villain, and I had a reliable plan for rescuing Olly forming in my head. All we had to do now was stroll to the end of the Path of Heroes and pop through the Fire Exit in time for brunch!

33

8:59 a.m. Friday

1 hour and 1 minute until Eternal Damnation

The Razor-Elbowed Glockenpard guarding the Tenth Task was truly terrifying. It was more hideous than the dinosaur-buffalo-supply-teacher-mutant of the Sixth Task. More disturbing than an exploding grandparent. More horrific than the sight of a T-Rex about to rip your best friend's head off in slow motion . . .

I sauntered past.

My plan for rescuing Olly from *Beneath* was all set up. And now, in honour of my Loyal Sidekick's noble sacrifice, I must fulfil my destiny. And I must do it exactly as he had taught me: lazily, skiving whenever possible, not taking things seriously . . .

For now, more than ever, I was certain that Olly had led me to Inlightenment. After all, I'd taken a mad risk which had made me FLY – so his skiving theory MUST have been *the truth that fear had hidden within me*. It wasn't what I'd been expecting, but hey – it sure made things easier.

'None shall pass!' boomed the Scraggle-Toed Bogflopper guarding the Eleventh Task.

'Hiya,' I said, wandering past.

Not Bothering really was the answer! It worked every time!

Look at the Home for Failed Heroes. All that running around, chasing crumbs, getting depressed by messages on armchairs – and I'd have been better off *Not Bothering* to go in!

I nodded casually at the triple-headed spider-shark guarding the Twelfth Task, and half-ignored the army of fire-breathing duck-kittens offering me another chance to complete the Fourth Task. As their quack-purring faded into the distance, the path curved round the mountainside, zigzagging upwards. My feet ached and Malcolm was grizzling, but we were nearly there. We *had* to be! But before we reached the end, I needed to hear –

Phoop! Phoop!

YES!!! My plan had worked!

I waited for the whistling policeman to catch us up.

Obviously I wasn't going to let Olly *actually* sacrifice

himself. *I* didn't want him to, and I don't think he really wanted to – and the middle-aged man jogging up the path certainly didn't want him to.

After I'd flown up from *Beneath*, I knew I needed a different, more reliable way to rescue Olly. I needed help. But who could I call? A friend? The police? Someone's dad? Or how about my *friend's police-dad* who'd been searching for him for thirty years???

Yes. The ideal person for this rescue mission was somewhere nearby, patrolling the Path of Heroes, looking for emergencies. But how to contact him? I considered calling the emergency services – but if I told them I was in the Land of the Dead, they'd think it was a hoax call, and hoax calls to the emergency services made people die, and the boy who needed rescuing was already dead, and the police officer who needed to rescue him was also dead . . .

And that's when I had my genius idea. All I needed to do was *commit a crime*. Olly's dad would track me down in no time, just like he'd promptly reported the illegally parked moon-buggy, and swiftly investigated the illegally dumped gym equipment. And I had the perfect crime in mind. One I knew would bring Sergeant Polliver running.

Littering.

As I'd continued my quest along the Path of Heroes, saying hi to the Beast Guardians and ignoring the Tasks, I'd *littered*. I'd torn page after page from my maths book and chucked them over my shoulder. I'd ripped and torn and shredded, and I'd scattered the fragments to the winds. I'd littered and littered, until there was no possible chance Sergeant Polliver could let me get away with it –

'Freeze! Don't move! Hands up!' yelled Olly's dad, struggling to catch his breath after the uphill jog. He surrounded me and Malcolm with blue and white POLICE tape, containing us in our own little crime scene.

'Hello,' I said.

'Nee-na!' said Malcolm.

'Yes, well. Good morning again,' said Sergeant Polliver, raising his notebook and pencil into action mode. 'Now, it would appear you have found the missing infant. Is that correct?'

'Yes, officer,' I said.

'*Yes. Off. Ic. Er,*' he wrote. 'And the child snatcher?'

'He . . . made a swift exit,' I said.

'Escaped, eh? Hmm.' He lowered his notebook and looked at me kindly. 'Don't worry, miss, I'll send the chopper out – they'll track him down in no time. Now, I wonder if you might know anything about another incident?'

Olly's dad held up an evidence bag stuffed full of ripped pages from my maths book. I felt terrible he'd had to pick it all up – but I was glad he had, because the thought of all that mess really bothered me.

'Yes, the littering,' I said. 'You got me: I confess. And

thank you for picking it up. But I only did it so I could talk to you. Olly needs your help.'

'*Oliver?*' Sergeant Polliver was so shocked he nearly dropped my litter.

'The trouble is,' I explained, 'he thinks you want to throw him in a police cell to teach him a lesson.'

'Why would he think that?' he asked, looking confused and hurt.

'Is he wrong?'

'Of course he's wrong. I'm his dad!'

'But you *have* been chasing him and blowing your whistle –'

'I want to give him a hug!'

'But can you see why he might not think that?' I said. 'Maybe if you approached him more slowly, without blowing your whistle, not in your uniform . . .?'

'I like my whistle!' he said, placing a protective hand upon the left breast pocket where his trusty whistle lived – just over his heart. 'Look, I spent thirty years waiting for Olly to come down here so I could say sorry. Thirty years! I knew he was hiding from me up there – I knew he thought I'd be cross, but I just wanted to see him and explain . . . You see, it was my fault we both died. When I climbed up after him, I scared him – he panicked – we both panicked.'

'But *he* thinks that *you* think it was *his* fault! You really need to talk.'

'I *tried* to explain,' said Sergeant Polliver, as a pair of chubby Regrets plopped on to his shoulders. 'When Oliver finally came *Beyond*, I went to meet him – as his Guide. But after thirty years of sadness, the feelings were just too much. We never had a lot of training on feelings at Police Academy. I'm afraid the emotions overwhelmed us both. We couldn't speak, didn't know what to say. Then he ran away again! It broke my heart.'

Well, this story was breaking my heart too. But time was seriously running out for me and Malcolm, and I really needed to get on with my quest. I just didn't know how to break the news; how to tell this heartbroken father that the son he'd been trying to hug for thirty years had plummeted into the bad bit of the afterlife.

'So you've got access to a chopper,' I said. 'That's a helicopter, right?'

'Yes. Why? What's happened? Is it Olly? Is he in danger? Has he fallen? He's gone over the edge, hasn't he? He's *BENEATH*!!!'

Phew! He'd worked it out. Perhaps *falling off* was a fairly routine catastrophe on this precariously narrow and gloomy path full of monsters.

Sergeant Polliver knelt in front of me. 'Where did he fall? I'll go down there. I'll get him back!'

'Yes!' I said. 'You will! You must! But just . . . calm down a bit first. The last thing we want is for this to be like the pylon accident all over again. So just CALM DOWN! And whatever you do, DON'T REPEAT 1989.'

'You're right. Panic is the enemy!' He took a deep breath. 'I should never have followed him up that pylon. I scared him, and that's why we both died. I know that. But I couldn't leave him up there! And I won't leave him . . . *down there.*'

'Okay,' I said. 'Go after him. But be careful. If you both end up trapped *Beneath*, Olly will blame himself again – and it'll be just like now, but worse. Because you won't just be sad, you'll be torn to pieces by Resentful Beasts in slow motion forever – AND sad.'

'I'm coming, son!' Olly's dad yelled into the abyss. 'I WON'T LET YOU DOWN THIS TIME!!!'

Sergeant Polliver was really making up for all those years of not expressing his feelings.

'Okay, I'm ready,' he said, sniffing thirty years of sorrow up his big policeman's nose, and puffing his chest out proudly. 'I'm an officer of the law, and I'm Olly's dad. Now tell me where he fell, and I'll rescue him.'

'He fell between the Home for Failed Heroes and the Tenth Task. There were electrified spikes, and nettles, and those extinct crocodiles – you know, the extra-long ones – and lava, and some of that illegally dumped gymnastics equipment . . . and when I last saw him, he was about to be savaged by a T-Rex.'

Sergeant Polliver swallowed and nodded bravely. 'Thank you, Miss – I'm sorry, I never even asked your name.'

'Harley,' I said. 'Harley Lenton.'

'Thank you, Harley Lenton. Olly is very lucky to have you as a friend.'

There must've been a little gust of wind at that moment, because some grit blew into my eyes and made them water. I blinked and dabbed them with my sleeve.

'If you see Olly first,' said Sergeant Polliver, handing me his whistle, 'blow this. It's like the Batman signal.'

'Okay,' I said, taking the whistle.

'Good luck with your quest, Legendary Hero.'

'You too, Sergeant Polliver. I hope you don't get dragged into an eternity of suffering.'

Olly's dad tapped his trusty notebook and struck a middle-aged Hero pose. 'All in a day's work.'

Sergeant Polliver was putting a brave face on, but getting those Resentful Beasts to respect the law was going to be tough – even with a helicopter and a truncheon. I watched him jog down the path, then turned and ducked under the cordon.

The Serpent of a Thousand Nightmares guarding the Secret Bonus Thirteenth Task was half a mile long and in a very bad mood. As I swept aside its sinister spirals, it hissed menacingly then slithered off in a sulk. And when the Path of Heroes was no longer clogged up with half a mile of slippery Bonus Beast, I could see that we'd done it – reached the end – completed our journey.

Like true legends.

I was too exhausted to dance or even smile, but I attempted a feeble high five with Malcolm, then flopped against the wall.

'Woo-hoo,' I sighed, slightly wishing I had a party popper, but also glad I didn't have to go to the effort of pulling its little string. If only Olly was here, he could've done one of his celebration yo-yo moves, like the Webbed Cradle or the Sick Spinner. Or maybe even a cheery song. '*Bish . . . bash . . . bosh . . .*'

I sighed.

Anyway, it wasn't party time yet. I still had to work out which of the three doors in front of us was the Fire Exit.

34

9:18 a.m. FRIDAY

42 minutes until Eternal Damnation

Three doors. One of them would lead us Back to Life. The others . . .

This was so like the *choice of three things* stuff that always happened to those Legendary Heroes. In fact, Craemog the Intrepid had been confronted with a decision exactly like this when the Night Knight trapped him in a tower with a golden door, a silver door and a wooden door. Using his cunning, Craemog worked out that the gold and silver doors led to Unimaginable Sorrow, and the wooden door led to Everlasting Bliss. But none of the doors in front of me were gold or silver or wooden. They were all standard uPVC with chrome-effect handles – just like the back door we'd replaced when Mr Purry Paws passed *Beyond*, and the cat flap became an unnecessary security risk.

Vileeda the Valiant had to choose between three *paths* – a dusty path, a rocky path and a leafy path. One of the paths led to the Suffering of Ages, another led to the Joys of Humanity, but I couldn't remember where the third path led, or which was which, and anyway they weren't doors.

More than anything, staring at these doors reminded me of days at Doreen's Door Shop with Dad. Doreen's Door Shop was full of doors, and I used to imagine that each door led to a different magical world. In reality, the doors in Doreen's Door Shop were all stacked up in a big pile, so each door could only lead to another door . . .

Mind you, if every door only leads to another door, maybe it doesn't matter which door you open first? Of course! The answer to this puzzle was the same as the answer to all things: *Not Bothering!* I'd suffered great hardship to learn the wisdom of doing nothing – I must remember always to use this special gift. I just needed to Not Bother thinking about which door to open.

I opened the door on the left. The little furry Beast Guardian of the First Task looked at me with big-eyed embarrassment and sank deeper into its candlelit bubble bath.

'Sorry,' I said, quickly pulling the door shut.

Awkward – but at least it wasn't the Suffering of Ages.

I knocked on the middle door. The Many-Limbed

Optimugoon opened it with a monstrous sigh.

'Read the sign!' it bellowed, pointing to the outside of the door with a clawed tentacle.

'There isn't a sign,' I said.

The Optimugoon looked at the door and sighed even louder.

'Where's the sign?' it roared.

I peered past its knobbly back into the room beyond. Several Beast Guardians were sitting around, drinking coffee and reading the papers. The Razor-Elbowed Glockenpard was filing its elbows. The Dreaded Polyops of Eastleigh was having a nap. Colin, the gangly stick-insect monster who I'd

threatened at the Second Task, was hunched over a sheet of A4 with a biro.

'Sorry, Les,' said Colin to the Optimugoon. 'It fell off earlier. I was just making a new one.'

Colin brought the new sign over and Blu-tacked it to the door:

STAFF ONLY. NO HEROES.

'Next door,' growled the Optimugoon, slamming the door in my face.

'Gaw! Gaw! Gaw!' said Malcolm, pointing to the third door.

'You reckon?' I said. 'Third time lucky, I guess.'

I pushed the remaining door open a crack. Peeping round the edge, I was relieved to discover neither a staffroom, nor a bathroom, nor a flaming pit of devils with pitchforks. The third room looked like an ancient library, with approximately a gazillion more books than the libraries at Kesmitherly and Risborough put together. I recognised a few of the titles: *A Hundred Heroic Escapades of Hallyria the Unrelenting, The Marvellous Voyages of Vileeda the Valiant, The True and Wondrous Adventures of Bilbamýn the Bold, The Chronicles of Craemog the Intrepid, The Fourteen Silken Horns of the Weaving Warrior* . . . In fact, *all* my grandparents' stories were here, alongside squillions and fadillions of other old books full of Heroes and quests, lined up on towering shelves that stretched out of sight.

As I wheeled Malcolm between these epically tall bookshelves, the trolley's squeaks and rattles sounded embarrassingly loud. I kept expecting to be shushed, but the only other person in the room didn't seem to have noticed us. She sat, hunched over an ancient-looking desk, writing in an ancient-looking notebook.

'Na-na! Na-na!' shouted Malcolm, eyeing up the book-lady's breakfast.

'Please, take it,' said the woman, passing me her banana without looking up. 'He sounds hungry.'

'Thank you.'

Malcolm stuffed his cheeks and giggled like a naughty hamster.

'Excuse me,' I said. 'I'm looking for the Fire Exit.'

'Ah, yes. You must be Harley the Legendary Hero.' The little grey lady folded her book shut and looked at me. 'I am the Archivist.'

'Hi,' I said, smiling nervously. 'Do you know where the Fire Exit is please?'

The Archivist continued to stare at me. 'You haven't done all your Tasks yet.'

'That's because I achieved Inlightenment,' I explained. 'I realised I didn't have to. Worked out it was all a trick. You know, a con. A red . . . herring . . .'

As the Archivist stared and stared, my confidence dried up. I tried to stammer on, but my words felt heavy and empty.

'Olly, my sidekick, showed me I didn't have to do it.' I stopped. It sounded like the lamest excuse for not doing my homework ever. 'I thought . . .'

'You thought what?' said the Archivist, peering over her spectacles.

'I don't know,' I mumbled.

The Archivist sighed. 'You thought just because there was no one to make you do it, you didn't have to do it.'

'No . . .' I said, not entirely truthfully. 'I thought I'd achieved Inlightenment.'

'Were you flying?'

'Sort of,' I said.

The Archivist gave me a withering look. It reminded me of how Mum and Dad looked at me during the Bad Times. Disappointed but unsurprised – as if failure was all that could be expected. Because of course I hadn't flown, not really. I'd bounced on a trampoline. And that meant I hadn't really achieved Inlightenment, which seemed embarrassingly obvious now. Why on earth had I listened to Olly's stupid suggestion to skip the Twelve Tasks?

'You'll have to go back and complete them,' said the Archivist, methodically peeling a satsuma. 'Can't let you through otherwise.'

'Please!' I begged. 'We've only got a few minutes until

we're trapped forever, and our parents will be waiting for us and they'll blame me and – *pleeease*! – Malcolm needs a clean nappy, I need to brush my teeth, we both need to be *alive* again . . . *Please* can you just let us through, *please*?'

'Don't beg, Harley, it's undignified. You're a Legendary Hero, remember. Show some respect for the job.'

I was silent, fighting back the tears.

'Now I'm sure you've had a very difficult journey, even without bothering to complete the Twelve Tasks. But getting all emotional simply won't help matters. Would you like a satsuma?'

I wanted to throw the stupid satsuma at the stupid Archivist with her stupid book. But I also wanted to eat the stupid satsuma, so I did – 'Zu-ma! Zu-ma!' – sharing it with Malcolm.

'Now let's see,' said the Archivist, flicking back a few pages to check her notes. 'You completed the first three Tasks, then you skipped the fourth and went straight on to the fifth. You're not the first to have had that experience after the Temptation. Jonab the Good, Chakof the Virtuous, and Dishnal the Righteous were all caught out by that one. Of course, it wasn't a pizza in those days.'

'How do you know so much about me, and all this lot?' I asked, gazing round at the looming bookshelves.

'I am the Archivist,' replied the Archivist. She looked at her watch and frowned meaningfully. 'Might I suggest you pop back rather *urgently* to complete these other Tasks? Most of them will be closing soon. We've all got homes to go to.'

Well, I seriously doubted Dinosaur-Buffalo-Supply-Teacher-Mutant and the Serpent of a Thousand Nightmares had anyone waiting for them at home. And I was dead certain this moany old library woman wouldn't be missed by whoever *she* lived with. Plus I knew for a fact that most of the Beast Guardians had closed their Tasks already, because I'd just seen them lounging around in the staffroom. But none of this made any difference anyway.

'I haven't got time to go back,' I said. 'We need to go through *now*.'

'I can't let you through,' said the Archivist. 'Even if I wanted to take pity on you, I couldn't let you through. It's an automated system. The Fire Exit only appears for a True Legendary Hero who has passed along the Path of Heroes and completed the Twelve Tasks. This is the way it has always been: there are no shortcuts to Heroism. You can't simply stroll along without doing anything and assume everything's going to be fine at the end. It's no good looking cross about it, Harley. Here, have a plum.'

Where this plum may have ended up, History will never know. Fortunately for the Archivist, just as I was preparing to use the unwanted fruit to express my rage, my Loyal Sidekick turned up.

35

9:29 a.m. FRIDAY

31 minutes until Eternal Damnation

'Harley . . . arley . . . arley . . .'

Olly stumbled towards us and collapsed at my feet, too weak to go on. His clothes were torn, his face was cut and bruised, he was barefoot and exhausted. Most disturbingly of all, his right hand was missing, severed at the wrist. I winced, turning away from the blood-soaked stump, trying not to imagine the pain and horror he must have suffered at the jaws of a gazillion ravenous beasts –

'Vroom! Vroom!' he yelled, poking his hand out from his sleeve. 'Ketchup! Ha ha ha ha! Tricked you! Oy! Oy! Oy! It's just ketchup up the sleeve, Harley-arley-arley! Vroom! Vroom! *VROOM!*'

Well, the Archivist loved the severed-hand-up-the-ketchup-soaked-sleeve joke, and so did Malcolm. They giggled and giggled like it was the funniest thing ever.

Personally, I didn't think it was that funny. Though I *was* relieved he'd avoided being eaten by the T-Rex. Presumably, he'd also avoided being rescued by his dad.

'You must be Oliver – the Loyal Sidekick!' beamed the Archivist, like a proud auntie.

'At your service, madam!' said Olly, bowing and curtseying and doing a little twirl. 'Have we done it, then? Finished the Path of Heroes? Are we gonna be in one of them books?'

'Maybe,' said the Archivist, her grey eyes twinkling at Olly. 'Tell me about your escape from *Beneath*.'

Olly didn't need to be asked twice. As he launched into a ridiculous story about summoning the beasts, the Archivist grabbed her tattered notebook and wrote it all down. She *oohed* and *aahed* as he described the improbable kindness of a pack of bears, the implausible generosity of a pterodactyl, and the entirely doubtful decency of a troupe of trampolining tigers.

'Is any of that true?' I asked.

Olly shrugged.

'Never mind that,' said the Archivist, gesturing for him to continue. 'Go on, go on!'

'Okay,' said Olly. 'So then this penguin with a jetpack –'

'Why are you writing this down?' I said. 'It's clearly nonsense. He's making it up. He always makes things up.'

'Someone's jealous,' muttered the Archivist. 'You were saying, Oliver? A penguin with a jetpack . . .'

'Yeah,' said Olly, sounding a bit less confident now. 'Well, this penguin, she used to be an opera singer . . .'

'Oh yes, I like that,' muttered the Archivist. 'That's very good. Go on!'

'And she married a mongoose whose uncle was an admiral in the navy. No, that's silly. Let's say the penguin lived in a gingerbread igloo . . .' Olly stopped talking and watched the Archivist feverishly scribbling his improvised nonsense on to a clean page of her notebook. 'Look, Harley's right,' he said sheepishly. 'I am a little bit making it up.'

'See?' I said. 'He makes everything up.'

'Every story can be improved with a little embellishment,' said the Archivist.

'But this isn't a story!' I said. 'This is *real life*. You're recording what *really happened* when Oliver the Loyal Sidekick escaped *Beneath*! Future generations will try and learn from this story – I mean . . . okay, not *story,* well it is a story, but . . . look, if you don't tell it properly, it gets confusing.'

'You just have to find the deeper meaning,' said the Archivist.

'Oh, come on!' I said, exasperated. 'That's the sort of

thing a teacher would say – and not a good teacher like Miss Delaporte. Why don't you just write down what *actually happened*? Like, probably, more likely, Olly was being chased by his dad in a helicopter, and he was so desperate to get away, he climbed out of *Beneath* like a boy up a pylon.'

'Ooh yes, I like that,' said the Archivist.

'You can't write *that* down!' said Olly. 'That's personal stuff. You can't put things like that in a book!' He turned to me with a wounded expression. 'I told you that stuff about my dad in secret.'

'Yeah, well – the truth *matters!*' I said, unmoved by his sad puppy eyes. 'Being *right* matters. Saying stuff just because it sounds good is irresponsible. Being wrong is dangerous!'

'What do you mean?'

'Me and Malcolm are trapped here because of your stupid plan to *not do* the Tasks!'

'Oh,' said Olly.

'A Legendary Hero cannot blame her sidekick for her failure, Harley,' said the Archivist. 'This young man volunteered to assist you. He threw himself into the jaws of death.'

She gestured to the dusty books surrounding us.

'Many Heroes have succeeded. Many more have failed. Tixeelix the Unready fell *Beneath* and was never seen again. Tonzilla the Unprepared was swept away in a devastating tornado created from the turmoil of her own mind. Hapnoweed the Spontaneous went completely the wrong way – never even found the Path of Heroes. These, and hundreds more, failed in their Noble Quests. But not one of them blamed their sidekicks. And not one of them failed simply because they chose to *not bother* doing the Tasks.'

'It was *his* idea!' I said, pointing an accusing finger at my Loyal Sidekick. 'I've never skived anything before in my life. I only did it because *he* got away with it!'

'So if he told you to jump off a cliff –'

'Yes! Yes, I *did* jump off the cliff because he did! I thought he'd led me to Inlightenment! I trusted him – and now it's all gone wrong, just like *Before*.'

'Don't be like that, Harley-arley-arley –'

'Just leave me alone, Olly.'

'No.'

'Okay, *don't* leave me alone. I don't care.'

We both huffed and sulked, and tried to ignore the fact that the Archivist was enthusiastically writing down everything we said.

'Why would you achieve Inlightenment by listening to me anyway?' Olly asked. 'You're the Legendary Hero; I'm just a salt of the earth wheeler-dealer yo-yo master!'

I walked away and pretended to look at the books.

The Archivist was right about one thing – it wasn't Olly's fault. In my heart, I'd known all along that skipping the Tasks was wrong. Skiving wasn't the answer, any more than violence was. For a moment it had made things look easier, so I'd been tempted. But I knew hard work was the only true path – my parents had worked hard to teach me that unhidden truth.

So much for Inlightenment. Maybe it'd come when I was old and wise.

Mind you, even if I had stopped to do all the Tasks, I would've run out of time and failed anyway. Failure was my destiny. It even said it on an armchair.

But it absolutely wasn't Olly's fault. And he really had thrown himself into the jaws of death, and crawled for hours in a sleeping bag, and cheered me up, and listened to me complain. And it was wrong of me to blame him for everything *Before* too. Dropping that watermelon, melting Mum's shoes – we'd done all those things together. Just like we'd travelled through the underworld together.

I thought about saying all this to Olly, but I didn't really know how. I got what Sergeant Polliver meant about feelings that stopped you from talking.

Why was life so complicated? I stared at the books in front of me, envious of all those characters with their stories mapped out for them, page after page. They didn't have to worry about what to do next or how to be good. Their futures had already been written – and not just on an armchair.

Not that you could trust them or their stories. Fake Heroes pretending to be brave, depressed monsters pretending to be scary . . . How was I supposed to "look for the deeper meaning" in a load of made-up stuff that had been flung together just to sound good?

Take this one, for example – *A Hundred Heroic Escapades of Hallyria the Unrelenting* – which began with Hallyria slipping all the way down Mount Ambivalence and landing in the Sea of Confusion. What did that have to do with anyone's actual experience? Or this one next to it, about Big Musclius the Confident who inherited an enchanted throne which magically transported him to a land full of monsters. Imagine that! Or this one, about Bilbamýn the Bold who discovered the Elixir of Death –

Hold on a minute. Now that I thought about it, Big Musclius the Confident's enchanted throne did sound quite like the caravan toilet. A lot like it, actually. And Hallyria's slippery mountain experience was *very* similar to the Flume of Infinite Terror . . .

Suddenly, all the stories came flooding into my mind in a great torrent of epic deeds, and I realised . . . It was all here! It was all here, and it had been all along! I could literally pluck any one of these books off the shelf and it would mean something! Look:

Bilbamýn the Bold discovered the Elixir of Death in a

bejewelled bottle, buried beneath the bones of a thousand warriors . . .

That was exactly like when I found the *Special Teabags* in a tin behind some biscuits!

The ancient alchemist transmuted the Elixir of Death in his magic cauldron . . .

Basically the same as when I brewed the *Special Tea* in a mug.

Bilbamýn the Bold poured the transmuted Elixir into the Bog of Uncertainty . . .

Just posh words for weeing it out into a spooky toilet!

It was all here. The Tea, the Portal, the Flume . . . Everything that *had* happened and *would* happen was all here – in the stories!

And now, I just needed to work out what should happen next.

I scanned the shelves for inspiration and found myself pausing at *The Moon Singer.* This was a story about a Legendary Hero who was cursed at birth so she could only wake at night. It was the ending that struck me – the part where she sang a haunting melody to summon the Moon Spirit, whose light she had forgotten to praise because she'd spent her whole life longing for the sun. I had a feeling that *meant* something.

On the shelf above, I spotted *The Chronicles of Craemog the Intrepid.* I smiled, remembering how much Nana loved the ending of the Fourteenth Chronicle, when the courageous honesty between Craemog and the Sky Wizard healed their ancient misunderstanding and 'brought forth tears of infinite joy'. Basically, it made them cry *so much*, and their tears were *so* powerful, that they parted the ocean. I grabbed the dusty book off the shelf and flicked through the pages to the end of the Fourteenth Chronicle. It was written in an annoying olden-days way – not good like how Nana told it – but it was still the same story:

> *And the intensity of Craemog's tears of joy did part the ocean.*
> *And lo, did Craemog and the Sky Wizard find safe passage between the very waves.*
> *And lo, passaged they forth amongst these very waves to their very homeland . . .*

'Tears of joy parting the ocean,' I murmured. 'Safe passage. Home . . .'

And suddenly, it hit me. A whole bunch of *deeper meaning* slammed hard into my brain – *WHACK! BIFF! KERPOW!* – and I knew what to do.

36

9:39 a.m. FRIDAY

21 minutes until Eternal Damnation

Possibly.

Anyway, I needed to get on with it because time was seriously running out.

'Olly, I'm sorry,' I said, turning to face my Loyal Sidekick.

'Yeah, me too,' he said, looking at his feet.

'No, I'm really, really sorry,' I said.

'Yeah,' said Olly, looking up. 'Me too.'

'Olly,' I said quietly. 'Close your eyes.'

Olly frowned. 'What you gonna do?'

'Just close your eyes,' I repeated. I stepped towards him. 'Close your eyes, and promise me you'll keep them closed until I say. I've got something for you. Something really special.'

Olly stood up straight, closed his eyes, and waited.

'What an ending!' said the Archivist, clapping her hands and stamping her feet. 'All that drama and conflict, and now the sweet reconciliation!'

She was scribbling breathlessly in her notebook, muttering to herself as she wrote. Hearing my own story in real time was like being bothered by a pesky kid who copies everything you say *everything you say* stop it *stop it* I'll tell Mum *I'll tell Mum* Mum! *Mum!* – but it was also kind of cool, like picturing your life as a movie.

'A moment of reconciliation,' the Archivist narrated, 'brought on by honesty and forgiveness, can reignite the Fire Exit, creating a gateway to *Before*. Even the Hero who has proven herself a failure in every other way can ignite the Fire Exit by conjuring up *tears of infinite joy . . .*'

I psyched myself up for an act of true courage. If this didn't work, there was no backup plan. I'd be trapped here for eternity, and my failure would be written down for the amusement of future generations.

The Archivist continued. 'Olly's heart was thundering in his chest. He'd stood up to Harley, she'd apologised, and now he was ready for the ultimate reconciliation. He kept his eyes tightly shut, and awaited his reward: a kiss from Harley the Legendary –'

'You what?!' said Olly, opening his eyes and stepping back.

'Get lost!' I said.

'Was you gonna . . .?'

'No way!' I yelled, glaring at the Archivist. 'Look, just close your eyes again, and ignore *her.*'

The Archivist glared back, then returned to her narration.

'Once again, Oliver closed his eyes and awaited his destiny. Suddenly, he was startled by a shrill shriek. The pounding of his heart grew louder and louder, pummelling him from above, like a tornado trying to flatten him. Still he kept his eyes tightly shut, until a pair of arms – bigger and stronger than he'd expected – grasped him in a forgiving embrace . . .'

'Dad?'

'Olly!'

'*Dad!*'

'*Olly!*'

'I'm sorry, Dad!'

'*I'm* sorry, son!'

Olly hugged his dad as *tears of infinite joy* rolled down their faces. I put the whistle back in my pocket and watched the parked-up helicopter's rotor blades slowing to a standstill. A wall of flames erupted between us and everyone stepped back from the intense heat.

'The Fire Exit!' said Sergeant Polliver.

'What a legend!' said Olly.

'Impressive,' said the Archivist.

I shrugged in a casually Heroic sort of way – even though my heart was hammering at my ribcage like a woodpecker in a cake tin, and I was close to shedding a few tears of infinite joy myself. We were going home!

'The heart-warming reconciliation of father and son,' continued the Archivist, 'after so many years of misunderstanding, had reignited the Fire Exit. Here, finally, was the Door to Before. At last the Young Hero and her Innocent Brother could make their way *Back to Life*!'

But before I had a chance to ask what I was meant to do with this Fire Exit – which was a lot fierier than I'd expected – it sputtered and popped and fizzled out.

This was a *nightmare.* I literally only had a few minutes until Eternal Damnation!

'With only a few minutes until Eternal Damnation,' the Archivist resumed, 'the Young Hero was in turmoil. It seemed the long overdue reunion of the Loyal Sidekick with his estranged father wasn't enough to reignite the Fire Exit after all –'

'Yeah, yeah, we got that,' I said. 'Stop telling us what's already happened and tell me what to do next!'

'I'm not really meant to help you,' said the Archivist, putting her pencil down. 'However, these myriad dusty tomes,' she gestured to the books again, 'have made me very, very wise. So I'll tell you what I think.'

She cleared her throat.

'Yours is a tale of fortitude, courage and sacrifice. But it is also a tale of loneliness. At any moment, any one of us may be called forth for Heroism. Most of us won't feel ready – but if we reach out, those around us will come to our aid. We must let our friends and families in, or we shall be forever alone, watching other people's stories, instead of living our own. Our friends and our families will make mistakes, just as we shall – but we must not push them away. Together, we can all be Heroes.'

'That's what I've been saying!' said Olly.

'The courage to love and be loved is the greatest courage of all.'

The Archivist paused.

'Deep,' said Olly.

'Yeah, inspirational,' I said. 'But I just need to know what to *do*.'

'Your grandparents' stories weren't wrong – they just weren't *YOUR* story,' continued the Archivist, who seemed to be digging around for wise-sounding things to say now. 'On the Path of Heroes, *everyone* is a Hero! Apart from the Failed Heroes. And the Beast Guardians – they just work here.'

The Archivist stopped talking and began sharpening a pencil.

'Why don't you open your present?' said Olly, wandering over to the trolley and poking the big gift with a yellow bow.

'Because I'm desperately trying to escape Eternal Damnation,' I said. 'I'm not really in a party mood.'

'Yeah, but think about it – your grandparents wouldn't make you cart a big heavy box all the way along the Path of Heroes for no reason. It must be something useful. Maybe it's like a . . . I dunno – something to help you.'

I untied the yellow bow and Malcolm helped me tear off the wrapping paper. Inside was a box-shaped contraption with a small tap.

'Looks like a tea machine,' said Olly.

'Ooh, yes please,' said the Archivist. 'I'll take mine nice and strong, with a squeeze of lemon.'

I ignored her and flipped the box over, looking for any hint of usefulness. On the back, there was a customer services number. I got my phone out and called it.

A familiar voice answered.

'Good morning, you're through to Jeremy. How may I help?'

'J-Wolf?'

'Who's that?'

'It's Harley.'

'Harley the Legend? Safe. You back up already?'

I explained our predicament.

'Yeah, that is awkward,' said J-Wolf. 'I'm putting you on speaker now, okay? Here's some people wanna talk to you . . .'

And then Nana, Pops, Gran and Grandpa all said hello, and I said hello, and just hearing their voices again brought me a moment of calm in the madness.

'Do you like your present?' said Grandpa.

'I could see you weren't keen on the Gatekeeper job,' said Nana. 'So we got you one of these.'

'This will release you from your Visionary Duties,' said Gran. 'It will allow you to grow in whichever direction you choose.'

'You must tread your own path, Harley,' said Grandpa. 'Create your own destiny –'

'Yeah, sure, got you,' I interrupted. 'But what actually is it?'

'It's a Self-Service Tea Machine,' said Nana. 'Just set it up in the caravan and the Restless Souls can help themselves. From tomorrow, the Portal of Doom will operate without a Gatekeeper!'

'Automation!' said Grandpa. 'It's the future.'

'We thought this might be best,' said Gran, 'what with school and everything.'

Well, that really got me. They actually *did* understand me, and they weren't going to make me do that crazy toilet job in the caravan with all the dead people after all. I felt a great wave of gratitude and relief.

'It's state-of-the-art technology!' said Grandpa. 'Doesn't need filling up, or electrical power –'

'Can I just say . . .?' J-Wolf interrupted. 'I didn't actually *build* this one. This one is like, *recommissioned* from 1976. Ones I build are like, tiny, smaller than your phone. Mind-activated digital soul-adjusters, you get me? But this thing, this Self-Service Tea Machine is, like, old. Your granddaddies thought you was better with this one. It's classic, innit. Analogue.'

'They don't make things like they used to,' said Pops. 'Just look how sturdy it is! Go on, Harley, give it a whack.'

'Those modern "digital soul-adjusters" are too fancy,' said Grandpa, disapprovingly. 'You can't rely on them. But this machine will keep on going forever and ever and ever.'

'Unless you forget to wind it up,' said Pops.

'Me and Malcolm are stuck here!' I said, putting an end to my grandfathers' excitement about an unnecessarily massive and ancient machine I'd been forced to carry for miles. 'The thing is, I didn't quite manage to do *all* the

Tasks – I'll explain that another time – and so basically I had to find another way to light the Fire Exit.

'So I used the stories. And I worked out that Olly and his dad were like Craemog and the Sky Wizard who needed to be *courageously honest* with each other – but also Olly's dad was a bit like the Moon Singer because he'd forgotten the Moon Spirit while he was *longing for the sun* – as in SON, get it? – so they needed to be *reconciled to heal an ancient misunderstanding*, and Sergeant Polliver's whistle was like the *haunting melody* and the parting of the ocean was a bit like the Fire Exit, but with water instead of fire – and, anyway, it worked. But then the Fire Exit sputtered out, even though there were *gallons* of *tears of infinite joy* because those Pollivers really bawled their eyes out . . .'

I breathed.

'Clever!' said Pops.

'Very clever!' said Grandpa.

'Hmm,' said Gran. 'But perhaps you are forgetting whose story this is.'

Then she paused. A long, meaningful pause, like the pauses she used to leave during maths homework. A waiting-for-me-to-work-something-out pause.

'What does Olly's story tell you about *your* story?' hinted Nana.

And then, once again, it hit me. Understanding

smacked into my brain like a watermelon hitting concrete.

'I've got to make another call,' I said.

'Goodbye, Harley,' said Nana and Gran and Grandpa and Pops. 'Remember, we love you, and we'll always be here for you.'

'Love you too,' I mumbled, blinking away a tear of infinite sadness.

'And don't expect *too much* from stories,' said Nana. 'Sometimes it's nice just to paddle in the shallows, and listen to the splashing of the waves . . .'

Then the call ended, and I tapped my last missed call.

37

9:50 a.m. FRIDAY

10 minutes until Eternal Damnation

'Hello, Harley love,' said Dad.

'Hi, Dad. Is Mum there too?'

'Yeah, she's just here –'

'I've got something to tell you both.'

I took a deep breath and readied myself for an intense burst of heat.

'Mum. Dad. I'm not really in Frimpton.'

In the silence that followed, the Fire Exit sputtered to life. But it was a timid, hesitant flame, not much bigger than a candle. I needed to go further.

I took another deep breath.

'I'm in the Land of the Dead. *Beyond.*'

'We thought you might be, love,' said Dad. 'It *is* your destiny, after all.'

'My what now? You *knew*?'

A breeze came from nowhere and snuffed out the flame.

'Well, we knew you were destined for something,' said Dad. 'And when we tried calling yesterday and you didn't answer, we came over to the caravan – and we sort of worked it out.'

'You *worked it out*?'

'We're all Visionaries in this family, love.'

'I'm sorry we never told you,' said Mum, 'about the Portal of Doom and so on. We were always going to – just as soon as we felt you were old enough.'

'We were just trying to protect you, love.'

I was too shocked to notice the Fire Exit had reignited and was now the size of a microwave.

'So, all along, you knew I'd one day have to . . . do a *quest* or something?'

'Well, yes,' said Mum. 'But these prophecies are very vague. We didn't expect you to be risking Eternal Damnation. We'd always hoped your Visionary Destiny might be something a bit easier – like feeding a Restless Soul's guinea pig for the weekend.'

'But you never saw Olly, right?' I asked. 'Because he's so good at sneaking –'

287

'I'm the Master Sneaker!' Olly interrupted.

'Yeah, he was sneaky,' I said. 'And that's why you thought my behaviour was so outrageous, yeah? Because you assumed it was just me on my own? And that's why you agreed with Miss Stemper about the counselling and the exorcism . . .?'

An awkward silence.

'*We* could see Olly,' said Dad, after a while. 'But your friends couldn't. So we pretended not to notice him sneaking noisily about. We went along with the imaginary thing to try and make life easier for you –'

'You knew?!'

'We had to tell you something –'

'You could've told me the truth!'

That made them go quiet again.

'It's because we knew how hard it can be,' said Dad, after a brief silence. 'Trying to get on with non-Visionaries when you know you're different. We've always found it easier to pretend we're just like them. Imagine if I tried telling the lads on the darts team that I can see dead folk!'

'But you *should* tell them! Be true to who you are!' I said, as the flames grew higher. 'And you should've told me! And . . . wait a minute – you gave me *The Big Book of Legendary Heroes and Mythical Monsters from All Myths and Legends All Over the World Ever* – to make me think your own parents' stories weren't proper myths! And here they are, in BOOKS!'

I gestured wildly at the looming bookshelves and saw that Olly and his dad were watching me wide-eyed, popping the Archivist's grapes into their mouths like I was an exciting bit in a film.

'I'm sorry,' said Mum. 'That was wrong. We shouldn't have done that.'

'In fairness, though,' said Dad, 'you can basically stick anything in a book, so –'

'We were just trying to do what's best for you, Harley,' Mum interrupted. 'I suppose we thought that because *we* didn't really enjoy being Visionaries, and didn't want the whole Gatekeeper lifestyle, that we should protect you from it. But we should've explained it all sooner. Let you work things out for yourself.'

'Anyway, how're you getting on?' asked Dad. 'Have you made it through purgatory yet? I hear there's a lovely kiosk on the Road to the Back of Beyond –'

'Yeah, done all that,' I said. 'I'm just trying to work out the Fire Exit.'

'Oh!' Mum choked up. 'We're so proud!'

I could really feel the heat now, as the Fire Exit grew and grew – bigger than two, three, four radiators.

Olly stepped in front of me, tapping his wrist. 'Five minutes, Harley-arley-arley.'

I nodded.

'Mum, Dad,' I said. 'I'm going to put you on video.'

A moment later, my parents' distant, loving faces appeared on the screen.

'By the way, Malcolm's fine,' I said.

'Of course he is,' said Mum. 'He's with you!'

The heat of the fire was making my eyes water and I had to look away. Then I remembered that this was the whole point – so I looked back, and saw that Mum and Dad were crying even more than I was.

'Mama! Dada!' said Malcolm, as I held the phone in front of him. And now the tears of infinite joy were cascading down everyone's faces, and the Fire Exit was a raging inferno.

The Archivist dabbed her eyes with a handkerchief and returned to her narration. 'All that remained was for Harley to summon the courage to pass through the Fire Exit – for unlike family, the flames would never forgive –'

'Hold on,' I said. 'Are you saying I have to *walk through fire*? With *Malcolm*?'

'Well, you don't *have* to,' replied the Archivist, tartly, 'but it would be a rather disappointing ending if you stayed here after all this. The whole father-son reunion thing was inspired – a lovely twist! And then the counter-twist of admitting your failure to your parents, only to discover that *they* had failed *you* – yet the LOVE remained . . .'

'Who's this rabbiting on?' said Dad.

'I am the Archivist,' said the Archivist.

'I can't walk through fire,' I said. 'It's not possible.'

'I believe you can, Harley,' said Sergeant Polliver, looking down at me like the proudest uncle ever.

'Well, thank you, but –'

'Who's that, Harley?' asked Mum.

I swung the phone round so my parents could see the Pollivers.

'Good morning, Mrs Lenton!' said Olly. 'This is my dad. Dad, this is Harley's parents. They used to pretend I wasn't real.'

'Nice to meet you,' said Mum, awkwardly.

'Likewise,' said Sergeant Polliver.

'Look, I don't mean to be rude,' I interrupted, 'but can we save all this *pleased to meet you* stuff for another time? I've got a wall of flames to walk through.'

'You can do it, Harley-arley-arley! You can do anything!' said Olly.

'We all believe in you!' said Mum.

'You're a Legendary Hero!' said Dad.

'I appreciate all the support,' I said, 'but I think you're missing the point. I can't walk through fire. Nobody can walk through fire.'

'Hot hot hot!' said Malcolm.

'When you pass through the Fire Exit, you *will* burn,' announced the Archivist. 'But it won't harm you.'

'What does *that* mean?' I asked, exasperated.

The Archivist shrugged. 'You'll just have to try it and let us know. You're the Hero.'

'This is a terrible ending!' I moaned, as the eager flames jostled for pole position at the Harley and Malcolm barbecue.

'I don't like the sound of burning,' said Mum. 'Can't you let them off this bit?'

'Yeah, come on, Mrs Book Lady,' said Olly. 'Burning's a bit harsh.'

The Archivist ignored them and resumed her narration. 'It only remained for the Legendary Hero to summon the courage to pass through the Fire Exit. Yet at the very moment of truth, she revealed her one weakness: Harley was afraid of walking through fire!'

'That's not a weakness!' said Olly. 'It's common sense. Come on, you're not telling it right!'

'Fine,' said the Archivist, huffily crossing out the last line. 'Despite her courage and admirable *common sense*, Harley hesitated upon the threshold of returning to Life. Would she stumble at the last hurdle? Would she remain forever upon the Path of Heroes, like Idolicles before her?'

'Oy! Oy! Oy!' Olly hollered. 'You can't put that Idollopy

scumbag in Harley's story! That's exactly what he wanted!'

'FINE,' snapped the Archivist, scratching out the last line. 'As Harley prepared to pass through the Fire Exit, she reflected upon the honour of finally becoming a permanent member of the Legendary Heroes Club . . .'

'That's dead posh, that is,' said Dad. 'Come on, love – that's gotta be worth having.'

'You get a certificate,' said the Archivist, pushing a sheet of paper with swirly handwriting across her desk towards me.

'Really not bothered,' I said.

'Oh, Harley!' said Mum. 'A certificate would look lovely on the fridge.'

I grabbed the certificate, folded it into a paper aeroplane and launched it at the Fire Exit, where it incinerated on impact.

Mum sighed, Dad shook his head, the Archivist pursed her lips, and Sergeant Polliver tutted. Olly and Malcolm cheered and laughed out loud.

'Nice one, Harley-arley-arley!'

The Fire Exit began to shrink.

'It's getting smaller!' said Olly.

'Time is running out, Harley,' said the Archivist. 'It's now or never. If you go, and complete your quest, I promise not to place your poor behaviour on record.'

'Whatever,' I said.

'And I'll skirt over all the other failures too. All the bad attitude and showing off. I shall make you appear utterly Heroic. But you must go now. And you must go with dignity. Remember, the True Hero shall walk *slowly* through The Fire Exit, head held high, bold and unafraid, like a noble warrior –'

'What a load of ruddy nonsense,' said Dad. 'Listen love, striding nobly at certain danger might be well and good for those Ancient Warrior types, but that's not how we do things in Kesmitherly. If you want to know what your old dad thinks, I suggest you stick your head down and leg it.'

'Dad's right,' said Mum. 'Like that feller we saw stealing a quiche out of Meg's Mini Mart last week.'

I thought back to the shoplifter Mum was referring to. He was dead quick. Would've got away with it too, if it wasn't for that lamppost.

I tucked Malcolm under my hoodie, pulled my hood as far over my face as possible, and charged the trolley at the flaming wall. The last words I heard before being burnt to life were, 'Oy! Oy! Oy!'

But I was never sure whether it was Olly shouting them, or me.

38

10:00 a.m. FRIDAY

71 hours until the End of Half-Term

I tumbled into the caravan, slightly singed and gasping for breath.

'Not gonna lie, Maccy: that fire was *hot*.'

Dad unloaded a fire extinguisher all over us and Mum dived in for hugs.

'Harley! Malcolm!' she said, scooping foam off her children. 'I want to hear *all* about your trip.'

'Pop BAM! Gam BAM! Gampa BAM! Nana-Macca BAM! Arwee *BOING*! Dada PSSHH!' said Malcolm.

'That pretty much sums it up,' I said, removing the soggy, charred and partially unravelled Tunic of Qu'architi-Nu.

Then I played the video of Malcolm's first steps and Mum and Dad spent the next ten minutes trying to get him to walk again. But he just giggled at them like the whole idea was ludicrous.

BK poked his head round the open door.

'Hullo, pet. Sorry I'm late – hey! Malcolm!'

'Hi, BK,' I said, as my favourite Driver of the Dead swung a gleeful Malcolm round his head.

'You did it! All the way down and back up . . . Incredible! And you two must be Mr and Mrs Harley? Great kids you got – you must be so proud. Anyways, we best crack on, I am running very late today. I've got eight for you out here. Shall I bring them in?'

'Give us a minute, will you, BK?' I said.

'No-ooo-oo-oo-oooooo-ooo-ooo problem!' he crooned, stepping back on to the sunny heath.

I tipped the tea machine on to the caravan table and Mum and Dad and I set it up in no time, working happily together like the legendary DIY experts we were.

'Look at that,' said Dad, admiring the mechanics. 'Just wind it up, and off it goes. Classic!'

I hoped this clunky old contraption really was as reliable as some people seemed to think. A lot of Restless Souls were going to be relying on it.

I explained the new self-service arrangements to BK and handed him the keys to the caravan. He was disappointed there'd be no more Gatekeepers of Kesmitherly to chat to, but he took it in his stride. After all, soul-adjusting machines had already replaced human gatekeepers throughout most of the world; the technology had to come to Biddumshire eventually.

'I'll gi-i-iiii-ve you-ou-ou-oooo lot a lift!' he sang. Then he rushed the Restless Souls of the Hesitant Dead into the caravan, loomed over them as they queued for the tea machine, and shoved them one by one into the loo, to pass through the Portal of Doom to *Beyond*.

A few minutes later, he dropped us off in the village.

'Thanks for all your help, BK,' I said, looking up into his big face.

'No worries, pet. Any time.' He ruffled Malcolm's hair. 'See you, little man!'

We watched the ghostly coach shimmering off towards Risborough, then Mum and Dad turned and smiled at me for ages. Mum had paint in her hair. Dad had paint on his glasses. It was great to see them.

'We thought we'd do something to celebrate,' said Mum.

'Your choice,' said Dad.

'How about Splash Madness?' I said, for some crazy reason.

'Really?' said Mum. 'You're brave.'

'Well, she *is* a Legendary Hero,' said Dad.

'Good point,' said Mum. 'Splash Madness it is!'

I looked at my thumbs, already regretting my choice of reward trip. 'Maybe we could go after lunch?' I suggested, suddenly keen to delay it for a couple of hours.

'Ooh, yes!' said Dad. 'How's about a slap-up grill at the Ragged Goose? I've heard great things about the new menu.'

Five minutes later we were in the pub, sitting round our favourite table – the one with the view of Meg's Mini Mart. As we waited for our food, Dad went on about the roadworks on the bypass, Mum pretended to listen, and Malcolm slept. I was feeling restless. I went through the contents of my rucksack, psyching myself up for one final act of courage. Along with the Scroll of Reg Proctor, there was a policeman's whistle, an evil pizza crust, a lightly charred #legend badge – and my phone, with a message from an unknown number.

> OY OY OY!!!
>
> miss you down here but dont hurry back!
>
> good luck with making friends what aint dead ☺
>
> PS thanks for sorting me and dad out.
>
> your a LEJUND!

This was all the encouragement I needed. I got up and walked out the back door and into the Beer Garden.

The Beer Garden was a bench near some bins. Sitting on this bench, reading a book, was Bess, the landladies' daughter.

'Hi, Bess,' I said, Heroically.

'Hi, Harley!' said Bess, her face lighting up.

'Wanna go Splash Madness this afternoon?'

Bess hesitated. For a moment I felt I'd made a terrible mistake. I'd tried *overcoming my fear* and *placing my trust* – but I'd gone too far! It was too risky, too reckless, too foolish! And now I wished a Portal of Doom would open up right here and swallow me –

But then Bess said: 'Can I tell you a secret?'

'Yeah,' I said, my heart thumping like a rabbit on a space hopper.

'I'm a bit scared of Splash Madness. I read this news article about a boy who nearly lost a thumb.'

'I'm scared too,' I said. 'But I reckon we'll be all right. Can I tell *you* a secret?'

'Yeah.'

'I haven't done my maths homework.'

'Whoa!' said Bess. 'Me neither.'

'And . . . I can see dead people,' I said, seeing as we seemed to be telling each other everything.

'Cool,' said Bess. 'Hey, maybe we could do the maths homework together, after Splash Madness?'

'If we've still got our thumbs,' I said.

'And then you could teach me how to see dead people. And I could teach *you* how to do this.' Bess stared at me until her eyes shook and her ears wiggled.

'Deal,' I said.

'By the way, what're you doing Saturday?' she asked, as we headed back into the pub. 'Have you ever been to Frimpton?'

'Not for a while,' I replied, peering down at my new friend and wondering why she was getting shorter – and why, in fact, everyone in the pub was getting shorter too.

It was only when I banged my head on the ceiling, that I realised I was flying.

Meanwhile, a life and a death away, a little grey woman was climbing a stepladder. Each step led to another, until the ground below disappeared. Eventually, she reached a gap in the rows upon rows of books that filled the epic archive. Removing a leather-bound volume from her satchel, she slipped it into the perfectly sized space on the shelf. The Archivist had experimented with several titles for this book, her latest record of a Noble Quest. *Harley and the Wavering Trolley. The Boy in the Bag Beyond the Back of Beyond. The Caravan at the Edge of Doom. The Girl Who Would Learn Some Manners.* In the end, she left the spine blank, and simply attached a Post-it note with 'Harley/Olly/Caravan' scrawled on it. She could work on the title when it was finished.

Acknowledgements

Thank you to Hannah, my agent, for your wisdom, passion, calm and integrity. You plucked me from obscurity and now my book ranks 642,714 on Amazon's bestseller charts. And that's before I've even finished this page!

Thank you to Sarah, my editor, for navigating the whole process so smoothly from your hot and cold hamster attic. You've been amazing and I feel very lucky.

Honestly, Sarah and Hannah, it's been a perfect collaboration from my point of view, like when me, Tricia, Shabina and Phil taught Media Studies.

Thank you to all who made this book so shiny and enticing: to Janene for the inside, to Tom for the outside, and to everyone who cast a professional eye over the backside.

A great big special thank you to Olia. Your magical talent is a source of constant wonder and joy.

Thank you to the team at Farshore, especially Lucy, Lindsey, Liz, Laura, Susila and Ellie. Thank you to Roni, Rebecca and Aleena for comments gratefully received and reflected upon, and for a conversation to be resumed.

Thank you to Mary, Colette, Karen, Jack, Rachael, Rita, Chris, and Steve for getting excited so I didn't have to.

Thank you to Patience and Michael for always taking my silliness seriously.

Good luck to Bob. I hope none of Harley's adventure feels as frustratingly implausible as that Harry Potter and that Paddington. I look forward to hearing about any unrealistic parts you've spotted over a pint at the Ragged Goose in Kesmitherly.

At this point, I've mentioned enough people that anyone unmentioned can feel justly offended. Rest assured, I've got something even better lined up for you – yes, *you* – than some pages at the back that most people won't even read.

Thank you, Mum, for stapling two bits of paper I'd scribbled on into a book shape when I was small. Thank you, Dad, for everything Bunny Fred ever saw in the corner of his garage, and for bringing him out of hibernation for the next generation.

Finally, love beyond thanks to Tuuli, Lyra and Nicola.

For all our new stories, every day, forever.

Beast Guardian Employe

PLACE OF WORK:	
MAIN DUTIES / RESPONSIBILITIES:	

Name / Role	Image	Strengths
Beast Guardian of the Third Task		Really scary. Brings 14 centuries of valuable experience to role.
Beast Guardian of the First Task		Good ICT skills.
The Dreaded Polyops of Eastleigh (Beast Guardian of the Seventh Task)		Attention to detail.
Beast Guardian of the Sixth Task		Really really scary. Snappy dresser.
The Many-Limbed Optimugoon (Beast Guardian of the Ninth Task)		Scariest of the lot. Impressive efforts on co-worker relations and staff morale, e.g. setting up Swingball team.
Colin (Beast Guardian of the Second Task)		Outstanding commitment to corporate vision and values.

ath of Heroes, Beyond the Back of Beyond, Land of the Dead

upervision of the Twelve Tasks of the Legendary Hero

Areas of Concern	Recommendations and Targets
Inclined to emotional outbursts. Lacks motivation after 14 centuries in same role.	Join staff Swingball team.
Not scary or monstrous enough. Fluffiness / cuteness undermines corporate brand message. Poor communication skills due to lack of mouth.	Speak up during staff meetings. Practise looking menacing in front of the mirror. Join staff Swingball team.
Reluctant to engage with client base of Legendary Heroes. Accused of cheating during office hide-and-seek tournament.	Join staff Swingball team.
Personal hygiene issues. Anger management issues. Several violations of employee dress code.	Invest in massive toothbrush. Try breathing exercises. Join staff Swingball team.
No one wants to play Swingball with him. Maybe TOO scary? Needs to work on interpersonal skills.	Offer incentives for joining staff Swingball team, e.g. biscuits, lollies, promising to not growl at opposition players.
Easily intimidated. Fragile. Not scary.	Advised against joining staff Swingball team.

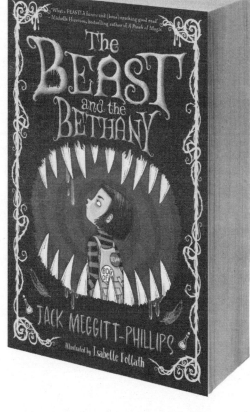

"SHARP, FUNNY AND BRIGHTLY IMAGINATIVE"
– JESSICA TOWNSEND, BESTSELLING AUTHOR OF THE *NEVERMOOR* SERIES

AMARI

AND THE

NIGHT BROTHERS

B. B. ALSTON

COVER ILLUSTRATION BY BRITTANY JACKSON

Welcome to the
Bureau of Supernatural Affairs